# TWO EYES OPEN

# TWO EYES OPEN

an anthology
compiled by MacKenzie Publishing


Contributions by

Chantal Boudreau, Amanda Crum, L.S. Engler,
R.A. Goli, Kev Harrison, S.T. Himmonds,
S.D. Hintz, Tom Johnstone, Billy Lyons,
Shelly Macaroy, Leslie Muzingo, Boyd Reynolds,
Leah O'Sullivan, Cassandra Williams,
Robb T. White, Monique Youzwa

*Two Eyes Open*
*Copyright ©2017 MacKenzie Publishing*
*Halifax, Nova Scotia*

*Edited by C.A. MacKenzie*
*Cover image by Angel Sharum*

*ISBN-13: 978-1927529300*
*ISBN-10: 1927529301*
*MacKenzie Publishing*
*August 1, 2017*

೮೦೮೪
𝓜𝒶𝚌𝓚𝑒𝑛𝔃𝑖𝑒 𝓟𝑢𝑏𝑙𝑖𝑠𝑕𝑖𝑛𝑔

# DEDICATION

*To Matthew MacKenzie Dickey,*
*who suffered a three-month horror story,*
*as did his family*

RIP
*April 28, 1980 – March 11, 2017*

"All I want is a heart"- The Tin Man

# CONTENTS

# PREFACE

This is MacKenzie Publishing's second anthology. *OUT OF THE CAVE* was published last year, and I'm extremely (no doubt prejudiced!) proud of these books.

As with the previous book, I received numerous submissions, and it was difficult to select the ones for this book. Several stories related more to a YA theme that would have been better suited to *OUT OF THE CAVE*. Others didn't fit my vision for the theme of this book.

Alas: I couldn't snare a famous person—or any person—to pen a foreword. Actually, to be honest, when an acclaimed author (no names mentioned) with the initials SK turned me down . . . well, I simply gave up!

Personally, this book is bittersweet. Matthew, my middle child, died unexpectedly in March from a rare cardiac sarcoma. I truly didn't know how I'd continue living, let alone finish this book. But here it is—and I dedicate it to him.

On the last page, check out the links. Follow MacKenzie Publishing to keep apprised of other projects, and "like" the Facebook pages.

Any errors are mine.

*Cathy MacKenzie*
MacKenzie Publishing
August 1, 2017

# RAGE
## Amanda Crum

Georgia summers are lush and suffocating, like the kudzu that grows wild and strangles anything in its path. When I was little, the consensus among my family was that heat was to blame for murder, adultery, and the general bad behavior of anyone over the age of three. None of us ever took to the summer months very well, even though the Garrets have lived in the South since before the war. It's the lack of sleep that does it. By August, the heat is so unbearable that all you can do is lie on sopping sheets with a cold washcloth on your forehead, waiting to die. When a storm whips up, you can smell it for miles—sweet rain mixing with bitter pecan trees. I've felt a storm coming for days. The air outside the window is heavy, clouds hanging low like a nursing mother's tits, ready to burst.

I luxuriate in the air conditioning and roll over in bed, cavernous without the weight of Ben on the other side. He's up with Austin, singing along with the radio in the kitchen. Saturday pancakes and fruit, half of which we'll have to clean off the floor. Toddlers and meals are exhausting. I close my eyes, stretch my toes beneath the sheet, consider touching myself. It's rare to have a moment alone, and my skin is still sleep-warm and soft. I think of myself at twelve or thirteen and waking up feverish. I was sexual at an early age, feeling for that little pink button to bring release every time I needed comfort. I reach down, pull aside my panties, and let my mind wander.

But something stops me. Something about the way the windowpane looks in the grey light of the room bothers me, and I don't know why. It's a slash of white in the gloom, a ribbon of reality on a day so overcast I can barely see the pictures on my nightstand.

When the woman standing in front of the window moves, I understand why everything looks wrong. The slash of white I had taken to be the windowpane was the sash of a diaphanous dress, high-collared and vaguely Victorian. My eyes open to capacity, bone-dry and crackling, filling my face, trying to reconcile what I'm seeing with what should be there. Downstairs, the Rolling Stones plead for shelter. She isn't all there, the woman at the window. She shimmers like an opal, dark hair shooting fiery strands into the ionosphere. I feel her hatred burning up the room, scorching the air with ruination.

My eyes tear and I blink against my will. When I look again, she's gone.

Normally I would take a hot shower to finish waking up, but I can't bear the thought of being alone one second longer. I throw off the sheet and crawl across the bed so I can get out on the side opposite from the window, moving as quickly as I can down the stairs without breaking into a run. If I run, I'll panic, and the story will come out of me in a flood and Ben will look at me like I'm insane or as if I'm a small child who needs consoling.

"Hey babe, I was just about to come get you up," he says without looking up from the griddle.

Austin is in his high chair, gleefully mashing strawberries between his hands. I bend and kiss the top of his sweet-smelling head, willing comfort from it. I can't talk about this.

"Sorry I slept so late." My voice is still thick with sleep, all the better to disguise everything else in it.

"You can sleep as long as you want, love. I just don't want you to miss Pancake Day."

He is preoccupied with flipping, watching the bubbles form amid puddles of browning butter. I wrap my arms around his middle from behind, breathe him in deep. Trying to forget.

"I wouldn't want to miss it, either," I say.

I hear his smile. "I made blueberry for you. I hope they taste all right."

"I'm sure they're perfect. They always are."

"Well, funny thing. I had to use some of the evaporated milk from the pantry because the stuff in the fridge had spoiled."

I pull back and frown. "Really? I just bought it on Thursday. Austin had some last night before bed, and it was fine."

"Yeah. I don't know. Maybe the wrong date got stamped on it or something. It wasn't just turned, it was chunky cottage cheese. I had to throw the gallon in the trash instead of pouring it down the drain."

And I think of her, rage burning her up from the inside out, watching me in bed.

*** 

I busy myself in the kitchen the rest of the morning, cleaning up and taking inventory of the pantry while Austin plays with his trucks on the floor. When Ben goes upstairs to shower, I brace, shoulders hunched almost to my chin, waiting for him to come back. Or her. But I feel nothing, no spark in the air, and Austin is happy. Too many books and movies have given me the unshakeable feeling that if she were here, the baby would see her even if I couldn't. We don't have any pets, but I'm willing to bet a dog would snuff her out, too. The incorruptible sixth sense.

"I'll call the roofer in the morning and set a date. Looks like we have another leak upstairs," Ben says when he comes down.

I glance out the window to the storm that's been winding up all morning. "Ever see that Tom Hanks movie *Money Pit*?"

"Yeah, but his wife wasn't nearly as hot as you." Ben stands behind me and rubs my neck, something he knows soothes me, and for a moment I feel a tiny flare of resentment. He can't allow me to feel what I feel. Everything has to be tamped down, intercepted. "Are you sorry we did it?"

"No," I lie. "I keep trying to see the beauty in disintegration. These old homes were built with such gorgeous details. It's just a little overwhelming, that's all."

3

"I know it is. But all we have to do is cross off one thing at a time, and before you know it, we'll have a beautiful old restoration that we can sell to pay off Austin's first car."

Another thing I secretly hate: the use of humor to make me forget what I'm upset about.

*** 

**I** shadow Ben the rest of the day, still unwilling to be alone with the baby in any of the rooms. I feel her here now, watching from a shadowy corner, and expect her to step in front of me every time I move.

Ben and I play games, build a Mega Bloks castle with Austin in the living room, and fool around on the couch after Austin goes for a nap. It's the first time we've been intimate in a while, and I cling to him, digging my nails into his shoulders. When I come against his hand, I remember wanting to masturbate when I first woke up and shudder, realizing she would have seen me, wondering if she's watching now. In the heat of the moment, I push it away, something I've been good at since I was young, and now that it's back, I numb it again. I tell myself that I'm spooked in this big old house. Stressed out, tired. I'd been half asleep when I saw what I saw. Or thought I saw.

We doze for a few minutes, lulling in and out of a light sleep soundtracked with lashing rain, and I'm so relaxed for the first time in months that it's easy to make myself believe it. There was no she.

After a while I get up, leaving Ben on the couch with his arm thrown over his face. The kitchen is the brightest room in the house because of the windows, and I head there instinctively, wanting a head start on lunch before the baby wakes. It's the first room we tackled upon move-in, stripping the old linoleum to find a lovely blond wood beneath. New fixtures and a massive island with a marble top give the space an updated feel without modernizing it too much. It was a labor of love, and we did most of it ourselves, stripping and sanding and nursing sore fingers at the end of the day. Ben went to the library and found photos in the archives of the home from the early 1900s so we had a point of reference, yet I didn't want to take it back to its original form. I couldn't say why, unless it was the natural ego of a restorer wanting to put something of herself into the work.

But if I'm honest, the house has had an odd feel about it since the first time we set foot in it. I chalked it up to the weight of history that any old home has—especially one built before the war—but now I'm not sure. And part of me—a small, small part—is curious about the woman I maybe saw. Curious, and angry that of all the things I've pushed away over the years, she's the most resistant.

It's not the first time I've felt haunted.

***

**I** expect to have an aversion to the bedroom when we go up, but the post-dinner cleanup, bath time, and baby-wrangling have left me more exhausted than usual. I undress, slide into bed, and into a surprisingly dreamless sleep before Ben finishes up in the bathroom.

When I'm jerked awake by the phone burring insistently, I shoot up in the dark, heart stuttering. "Hello," I say, my voice shivering from the weight of fear. Ben stirs beside me, and I glance at the clock: 2:17.

"Elizabeth?"

"Teresa?"

"I'm sorry to call so late. I just thought you should know, before someone else calls. Dad had a heart attack driving home tonight. He's gone."

I close my eyes. "Gone" could mean any number of things. He might have run off the road and hit a tree. He might have died before impact when his heart gave one final push against his ribs. He might have swerved his semi into the opposite lane and taken out a family in a minivan. I can't see it clearly, and I don't care.

The room isn't as dark now that my eyes are used to the dim light. Bulky grey shapes form in the gloom, the boxy reality of antique furniture that was once in another house, in another time. Who's to say what ghosts might come attached, trailing behind with every move like a dust-bunny? I think of her, the rage, and wonder where my father is now. Maybe she was a warning.

"Elizabeth?" Teresa says softly.

"I'm here."

"I'm sorry to wake you up. I just wanted to give you a heads up on the news. Mom will be calling as soon as she gets up."

"She sleeping with some help from her little blue friends?"

A pause. "Yeah. I thought it was best."

I sigh. "Thanks for the warning, Tre. I'll call you later."

"Goodnight, Beth."

I hang up, wishing I had a cigarette even though it's been years since I last smoked. Ben had been adamant about me quitting, even before we started trying for a baby.

"Babe? What's going on?" Ben rolls closer to me, snaking an arm around my blanketed legs. I'm tempted to yank them away from him. He fucking knows what's going on; he was twelve inches from the phone. Why does he feel the need to play dumb? I want to punch that placating note right out of his throat.

"My father is dead. He had a heart attack on the road."

"Jesus, I'm so sorry," he says. "Is Teresa okay?"

At the sound of my sister's name in his mouth I turn to look at him. "She's fine."

"Are you okay? What do you need? I'll call the roofers and tell them to postpone."

"I'll figure it out in the morning." I pull away and throw off the covers. "I think I want to go for a drive."

He sits up and switches on the lamp. "Are you sure that's a good idea? You're upset, babe. Come lay down, and I'll make you some tea."

"I don't want any fucking tea," I say softly. "I want to go for a drive. I'll be back in a while."

I throw on sweats, a tee, and old sneakers, and I watch him gape at me from the bed as if he's a fish out of water. It's dark downstairs and the woman could be anywhere, hiding around any corner, waiting for me, but I don't care. When I walk through a pocket of hot air on my way to the door, I don't even slow down, but it turns out she was ahead of me; sitting atop the car is a small bundle of feathers tied with a red ribbon.

Rage sneaks up my throat like bitter vomit and I spit, eager to have that taste out of my mouth. I don't want this here.

The car purrs under my touch, and I wind it up on the back roads, taking curves dangerously fast. Coming back from the convenience store, I smoke six cigarettes in a row, lighting the next off the embers of the last.

***

**I**n my dream I am fourteen, watching my first porno. I am pre-makeup and lean legs, flat stomach from a year of gymnastics. I lie on my teenage bed in the near-dark, waiting to feel something. Watching the screen as a man and woman appear and undress, the woman a petite tanned thing with a bruise on her ass, the man burly and hairy. His back is to me and when he pushes into her from behind, she looks coquettishly over one shoulder at him, glossy lips forming a perfect O.

My panties feel too tight and I move them aside, watching the age-old story unfold. My eyes are fixated on the screen, and when I'm about to come, the man turns around and winks at me. It is my father.

I wake with my heart thudding in my throat, lips dry as though I have a fever. The room is still dark, but Ben is gone. I throw off the covers and look around the room with tormented eyes, squinting against a headache to try and find her. It's hot, so hot I can barely breathe, and I know she's to blame.

But there is nothing to see. I sit, swing my legs over the side of the bed, and scrub my face with one hand. I'm slick with sweat. That dream. It eats at the edges of my brain, for all the world feeling like a threat. Tiny slices of daylight creep in around the heavy curtains that I notice for the first time are drawn. I slept through the night after all.

I sigh and stand to make my way to the shower, but a voice whispers, "Where are you going?" and I shriek, falling back against the wall and pulling the curtains open in my wake.

She's there—the woman, pale skin a riot in the near-dark, cold eyes surveying me. She's smiling, enjoying this, sitting on the edge of the bed. She's been there all along, next to me. I picture her placing a hand to my forehead like a backwoods preacher while I slept, guiding my dream along a track, burning me up with it.

I want to ask who she is, what she wants. Why she's here. I want to scream at her to fuck off, to stop torturing me. I'm horrified to see that her heart is visible in her chest, a red-black pump squeezing blue matter beneath her dress. She reaches and pulls my pillow closer to her, stripping off the casing without taking her eyes from me.

"I never could tolerate the cold. I used to sleep wrapped up in a quilt even in summer. Of course, our summers weren't half so hot as yours," she says.

I slide the rest of the way to the floor and scoot back against the wall on my butt, saying nothing, willing her to stay a distance from me.

She smiles and plucks a feather from the pillow lining, lets it fall to the floor. Another. Another.

"I was soft like you once," she says after a few moments, "but sometimes a woman has to harden her heart against the wolves. Sometimes rage is all we have left."

She pulls more feathers from the pillow, one by one, and drops them to the floor. A little pile has formed at her feet, a drift of white like snow or memories. I'm suddenly not sure this isn't a dream. Maybe I'm sick and having feverish nightmares. Maybe I'm dead, and this is Hell. How else can she know these things?

"I don't want to think about this," I say finally.

"Oh, but you must. You remember the feathers, don't you, Elizabeth?"

"No. No!"

"Yes, you do. It's in your eyes. It's been in your heart since your twelfth year."

"Why are you doing this to me? Why are you here?" I plead, holding up both hands palms-out as though to ward her off.

She looks taken aback, sitting so properly on the bed in her high-necked dress, a train of feathers puddling at her feet.

"I thought you knew," she says. "I'm here because you called me. You and your rage."

***

**I** walk downstairs slowly, still in my soaked T-shirt and panties. Ben murmurs on the phone while the baby babbles in the playpen. Outside the day is grey again, threatening more rain, enough to flood or make things clean. Maybe that's what we need, and I snort.

"Beth?" Ben calls, and then, quietly, "I'll have to call you back."

When he sees me standing on the stairs, I see what he's thinking as clearly as if he'd said it out loud. Sickly, sweaty, half-dressed, hair a mess, standing still on the staircase, and looking at nothing. He thinks I've lost it because my father is dead.

"Honey? Are you okay? Jesus, you're dripping sweat."

He moves toward me, and I back up a step. "Don't," I warn.

"Are you sick? What can I get you? I was just talking to Teresa about the funeral arrangements. I think everything is taken care of."

The thought of attending my father's funeral and seeing his heavily made-up face in an expensive coffin makes me want to laugh and gag at the same time. What comes out is a strange combination of both, and I half-fall to the stairs.

"Jesus, honey, let me help you back to bed." Ben reaches for my arm, and in that moment before I push him away, I remember being twelve and feeling my father's weight on the bed. I remember enduring silently when he bit down on his cries, smothering them with my pillow before throwing it aside, where it burst open and showered feathers. I remember filling up with hatred so potent it was almost tangible, a red and pulsating thing that never left, which burned a shadow on me so powerful it could curdle milk.

9

I look at my husband, and I recall, too, the way he casually said my sister's name even though he only met her once.

Once that I know of.

"Sometimes a woman has to harden her heart against the wolves," the woman said. "Sometimes rage is all we have left."

# SOUL CAKES
## Chantal Boudreau

"**Z**ebby, where you off to?"

Her father's dour voice made her jump, almost causing her to drop her basket.

"Bringing bread to Great-Great-Aunt Ruthie," she replied, trying to hide her fear. She glanced at him over her shoulder, and he frowned at her in return.

"Don't you take long. I expect you to be back in time to make the family dinner, and you have to prepare it early. Caleb's invited you to sup with him and his sister tonight. I want you to bring some over to him, too, as a gesture of goodwill."

Zebby shivered. She wanted to gag at the idea of courting with the man her father had chosen as her betrothed. Caleb looked like a dried-up old apple doll: crusty around the edges, scraggly hair and graying beard, and sun-damaged skin emitting a foul smell. The day they had been introduced, he had eyed her up and down with a caustic look and demanded what kind of name "Zebby" was. She had explained her father wanted a son, Zebediah, for a firstborn, and had been too impatient and stubborn to save it for the next in line when she'd been born.

Caleb had laughed at her predicament even though the choice of name had never been hers. His was a jarring, mocking laugh, loud and hard. He had said she may as well have been a boy, deserving of that name or worse, as scrawny as she was and not much to look at. Better yet to have named her after one of his hunting hounds, he had insisted.

If that was the case, why did Caleb always leer at her as if ready to pounce, his bleary eyes fixed upon her and his leathery lips curled ever so slightly? He seemed to find her as tempting as she found him disgusting, even if he claimed otherwise. Perhaps he had been putting on a show in hopes her father would up her dowry. It had never seemed right at all.

"I know, Papa. I won't be gone long. I'm just dropping this off before I go gather mushrooms for the stew. You know Ruthie can't cook for herself. She's old and sick. Me and the boys are all the kin she has."

"I don't see why she still gets to put any demands on this family. The only ties she had to us was your mama, and she's dead and buried years ago."

Zebby wanted to argue that her mother's passing didn't make Ruthie any less her blood kin, but she bit back the comment. She had learned at an early age that backtalk would earn a blow, truthful or not—another reason why she hated her current situation.

"The Bible tells us to be charitable," Zebby said instead, knowing this would have more sway with her father. Reminding him of gospel wouldn't prompt a slap.

He grunted and shrugged but offered no more objections.

Zebby picked her way through the swampy stretches between her house and great-great-aunt Ruthie's, fretting over the time she would have to spend with Caleb later that day. By the time she arrived at her destination, she had already worked herself up to tears. She couldn't bear the thought of marrying the man, let alone bedding him. The idea made her skin crawl and her stomach lurch.

The cottage's dim lighting caused Zebby to squint when she entered. Ruthie kept the windows shaded, insisting the sun's glare gave her headaches. Zebby found the old woman asleep in her rocker, huddled under her worn quilt despite the warm and stuffy room. Ruthie startled awake when Zebby closed the door.

"I brought you bread, Tante." That was how Zebby's mother had always addressed Ruthie, so Zebby continued to do so. "I'll leave it in your basket on the counter." Normally, she would have offered to tidy up and prepare a meal, but her father had made it clear she wouldn't have time to spare. When she stashed away the loaf, she absentmindedly brushed a tear from her cheek. The gesture wasn't lost on Ruthie.

"Have you been crying, chere?"

"It's nothing for you to worry about, Tante."

"Nonsense. What has you bothered?"

"I'm not exactly fond of the man Papa tells me I have to marry. He's old and foul, both in body and spirit. If I do anything to try to get out of it, I'll get beaten for it."

Ruthie frowned. "I'll never understand why your mama agreed to marry such a cruel man. But then again, she didn't come to me for advice at the time, either. I swear he was the death of her, not birthing your baby brother. She didn't have the will to fight when things went awry, thanks to your papa. But it doesn't have to be that way for you. You can get rid of him yourself—now, before it's too late. When's your next chance to prepare him a meal?"

Zebby felt blood sink from her cheeks and goosebumps rise on her arms. "Tonight. I'm making stew. What do you mean, get rid of him?"

"With mushrooms?"

Zebby nodded. "But—"

"All you have to do is pick a little of the wrong kind and slip it into his serving. I can show you a bad kind that looks like the ones good for eating," Ruthie offered, struggling her way out of her rocker.

"You mean poison him? I can't do that. It's a terrible sin. I'll doom myself to Hell, and he'll haunt me for the rest of my living days."

Ruthie cocked a silvery eyebrow. "I can't speak for your immortal soul, but I think rescuing yourself from a living hell is what matters at the moment. You can always work toward redemption after you've spared yourself from marriage to that man. As far as any hauntings go, All Hallow's Eve approaches. You can bake yourself a soul cake to offer up to his vengeful spirit. It'll put him to rest and you can move on with your life. Do you really want to ending up laying with someone like that and birthing his children? You'll fare worse off than your mother,

God rest her soul, and you know where a life of misery landed her. At least your father was close to her in age, not some old man after some fresh young thing and her dowry."

Conflicted, Zebby tried to brush off the remark about her mother. "Any woman can die in childbirth."

"But it's a lot more likely to happen when someone beats her regularly. Your papa broke her spirit. She might have been able to live through a hard birth, but she didn't want to fight for her life. She'd had enough of his cruelty. I'd wish she'd had the gumption to throw those mushrooms into his stew, once she knew his true nature. It started once his ego was wounded by the likes of you and it never stopped, even after she bore him son after son."

Zebby couldn't agree with Ruthie's suggestion, but she placated her by accompanying her to the mushroom patch. As they shuffled along at an arthritic elderly woman's pace, Ruthie insisted on rattling off the recipe for the soul cakes. "You remember that in case I die before the time comes. They only work on All Hallow's Eve, though. The spirit of the dead will come looking for you to deal with unfinished business. They take on animal form and hunt you out. You'll know it when you see it, and once you feed him the cake, he'll be done with you and the rest of this mortal realm. Then you're free until your papa dregs up some other unsavoury suitor."

After Ruthie showed her the poisonous patch, Zebby offered to walk Ruthie back to her cottage, but the old woman shook her head. "I've slowed you down enough. You get home late and your Papa will have your hide—before he sends you off to spend time with his wretched friend. Pick a few, then go find yourself some of the proper ones, over by the creek. Then get yourself home before he suspects anything or takes offense at your tardiness."

With that, Ruthie hobbled off. Zebby gathered a few of the toxic fungi in her handkerchief to keep them separate in her basket. She couldn't see herself committing such a terrible sin, but she might change her mind if desperate—and then her great-great-auntie's solution would do her no good if they'd been left behind.

Zebby was getting up from her knees and brushing away twigs and moss from her shins when a voice from behind her made her jump.

"I wouldn't pick any of those, Little Miss Zebediah. Those ones there are poison."

Zebby recognized the speaker, and her heart skipped a beat. When she turned to face him, her cheeks flushed and her skin prickled with delight.

"You think I don't know that, Master Maynard? I'm going to gather the good ones over by the creek. You can come with me if you like."

"I can't imagine a time I wouldn't like that, Miss Zebediah."

Maynard followed at a respectable distance, his presence lifting some of the darkness from Zebby's heart. He was the one young man Zebby would have been pleased to marry, but his father and hers were less than friendly, so there was little chance of that ever happening. She had considered running away with the lanky boy to avoid marrying Caleb, but if Maynard were willing that would only trade one big problem for many smaller ones, and they would never be able to return after eloping.

They talked, flirted, and laughed while Zebby gathered mushrooms, and when she started to leave, Maynard stopped her with a gentle hand on her wrist.

"Going so soon?" He gazed upon her with a longing that made her heart flutter.

"I have to. Papa needs me to make supper early today."

"You have to see Caleb tonight, don't you? I can tell by the sadness in your eyes and the tremble in your lip."

Zebby didn't have to say yes. An unspoken pain passed between them. She strengthened her grip on the basket before she turned and fled.

While she scurried home, she made a point of remembering everything she could about Ruthie's soul cakes. Her great-great-aunt was right. How was a life of misery a life worth living? She had changed her mind, after all.

She would not allow her father to force her to marry Caleb, no matter what it took.

***

Zebby carefully set aside the large tin of stew she would be taking with her, slipping the poisonous mushrooms inside. A part of her already felt guilty, not because the tainted stew would spell the end of her unwanted betrothed, but because she could not think of a way to stop his sister from eating it, too. Zebby had already decided she would take only a small portion and feign illness without consuming any of it. She could not come up with a plan that would prompt the spinster to set the stew aside that wouldn't deter Caleb at the same time.

Trying to ignore the butterflies in her stomach, she put on her best dress and loaded up her basket: flowers for Caleb's sister, a loaf of bread, and finally, the steaming tin. She made her way out the door without a word to anyone, but she did not leave unnoticed. She had taken only a couple of steps up the footpath when a hand from behind grabbed her painfully by the elbow and another yanked her basket from her hand.

"Where do you think you are going with that?" Papa sounded angry, and for a moment, Zebby was sure he had figured out her plan. Tears sprung to her eyes, and a lump caught in her throat. "Are you trying to insult Caleb and his sister with such a pittance of an offering?"

Placing her basket at his feet, he pulled out the tin of stew and replaced it with the small cauldron from the kitchen, which was twice its size. "Caleb's a big man. He doesn't pick at his food like a bird, like you do. You need to feed him, not starve him. Better too much than too little."

Zebby wanted to object but found it difficult to find her voice, let alone come up with a reasonable excuse. After he turned to go back into the house, she finally squeaked a protest. "The cauldron's heavy, and I have a long way to go through the woods—"

The blow from his open hand struck her before she finished her sentence. The force launched her into the dirt.

Her father scowled menacingly while he stood over her and shook his head. "What a shame you went and made me do that, and now your dress is soiled. But you don't have time to change it, so you'll go as you are and say you're sorry for being slovenly. No more sass from you. Pick yourself up and get on your way. No more complaints, either."

Dazed from the concussion, Zebby did as she was told, slinking off into the forest with the basket containing the small cauldron instead of the tin. Her cruel father had won again. Her plans for liberating herself from Caleb had been ruined.

But what would become of the meal she had been forced to leave behind?

***

Zebby opened the door shortly after the funerals to find Maynard, hat in hands and looking solemn. "I've come to bring you my condolences. Nobody should lose all their family like that—not all at once."

Her lip trembled when she tried to find her voice to answer. "I still have Ruthie," she managed to mumble.

"I thought you told me you could tell the difference between those mushrooms."

Zebby nodded, dropping her gaze to her feet. "It was all an accident." *Nobody but Caleb, and likely his sister, were supposed to die*, she thought, but she didn't share that with Maynard.

Denying it was the only way Zebby could sleep at night. If she accepted the blame, realizing she had caused the deaths of innocents along with the one who had wronged her, the guilt would have eaten her up from the moment she woke to the second fatigue claimed her. And that was without factoring in the excruciating pain she had caused them. She refused to imagine any of it, how they had probably writhed and clutched at their guts until oblivion finally offered sweet release, how they had struggled and moaned and prayed for mercy while they paid for their fatal meal of her mushrooms. If she had only been clear-minded and capable of considering the consequences to her papa's exchange, she would have admitted her desperate plot to her father and suffered for it. But she had been dazed by his blow and not thinking clearly.

"I wish it had been me instead of them—especially poor little Zeke."

Maynard sighed and hugged her. Zebby clung to him for solace and a sense of security.

She was doomed to Hell now. How could she redeem herself for five deaths when she had known two would be challenge enough? But Zebby would be haunted by them for a short time, for she would only have to wait until All Hallow's Eve and then her salvation would come in the ritual of the soul cakes. At that point, their spirits would pass to the other world, and she would find peace again, but it wouldn't spare her from the weighty regret of her wrongdoing.

"What's going to happen with Caleb?" Maynard asked

Her father's death meant Zebby was no longer obligated to marry his repulsive friend. All contracts void. None of her brothers were alive to renegotiate with him, either.

"Caleb won't bother me for some time. He won't even try to contact my next of kin, attempting to lay his claim, until the two-year mourning period is up. But I'll be worth more to him now. I come with more than just a dowry—I come with the family home. If I'm lucky, he'll decide he can't wait two years and move on. If not . . ."

Zebby gazed up at Maynard. She had not gone looking for him since her family's deaths, considering him partially to blame for her bad decision. Truthfully, none of it was his fault. As her late mother had liked to say, the heart wants what the heart wants, and despite tragic events, Zebby's heart still wanted Maynard.

"If he can't, you want to run away together, the way we talked about before your family died?"

No one could stop them. Zebby could court her beau in secret until her mourning time ended, and if Caleb came sniffing around again, she and Maynard could leave. She had already concluded this was what she should have done the first time, instead of panicking and following Ruthie's advice, but it was too late to change her mind. The damage had been done. All she could do was avoid making another mistake the next time.

Zebby nodded.

Maynard smiled. "I think I'd be agreeable to that if you'd be agreeable to leaving sooner. I can't promise you my own kin won't try to have me court some girl in the best interests of our family. That girl would never be you. If that happens, you'll have to be ready to leave with me then. It works both ways."

"I understand. And I would be, if it comes to that."

After Maynard left, Zebby felt a chill run through her. She sensed the spirits of her murdered father and brothers present in the house and had already gathered the ingredients needed for the soul cakes she had to bake to send them away once and for all. It was just a matter of waiting for All Hallow's Eve. Two more days, and all that would be left to torment her would be her own feelings of guilt.

***

Zebby sat on a stool beside the door leading out of her house, shivering and clutching her tin of soul cakes. The whispers that served as a constant reminder of her unsettled kin had faded with sunset. The eerie silence that accompanied the flickering candlelight seemed worse than their constant pestering. They would no longer be haunting her as they had before dusk but would actually be physically seeking her out, in some form or another, to try to take revenge. She could only hope and pray that the soul cakes would serve as sufficient solace for their restless souls—not that God would be listening to her after the sins she had committed. If her offering did not satisfy them, she would be surely doomed.

Part of her wished she had shared the truth with Maynard so she did not have to wait alone. She worried, though, that if he knew the facts—that the poisonous mushrooms were picked intentionally—he would lose interest in her. He was a good boy and wouldn't want to be associated with a family-killer, even a repentant one.

It was hours before the first revenant made an appearance. Zebby was growing drowsy when an agitated scratching started at the door. She was frightened to open it and face whatever was behind.

The creature on the stoop was something far smaller than she had expected, a weaselish beast with glowing red eyes that snarled and spat and bore its fangs at her as soon as nothing barred the way in between her and it. It reminded her, in some way, of her brother Calvin.

She quickly dropped one of the soul cakes at its feet and took a step back, cowering. It paused, sniffing at her offering. The moment the possessed beast snatched the gift in its teeth, Zebby slammed the door. It took several minutes with her back pressed against the wooden surface for her teeth to stop chattering and her heart to stop racing.

But that was only the first. More would come, and she knew it.

When the scratching began a second time, at least Zebby was prepared and far from drowsy. The wind had started to howl outside, so she did not hear it at first, but as the grating grew more frenzied, it caught her attention. The creature outside sounded larger than the first, which had been frightening enough despite its tiny size.

With one soul cake in her extended and shaking hand, Zebby threw open the door. A fox, eyes aglow, was perched on the stoop, hackles raised, ears folded, and tail thrashing from side to side. It looked as if it was ready to pounce and made her think of her brother Clem. She shoved the soul cake in its face, hoping to distract it from its attack.

Ruthie's recipe paid off again. The spirit-infused beast snapped up the small, round cake, almost taking one of Zebby's fingers with it. Its tiny, sharp teeth managed to pierce the skin, drawing blood before it left with its spiced prize.

Zebby did not investigate the damage before slamming the door. Tears added to her gasps and shakes, and she worried what would come next. The creatures grew more frightening with each new arrival, and she wondered if she could offer up the soul cakes fast enough to avoid anything worse than a nipped finger.

She did not have much time to think this disconcerting idea through because the next arrival did not present itself with subtle scrabbling or scratching. Instead, the whole door shook when something heavy beyond jostled it with full weight. Zebby wasn't sure what frightened her more, facing what stood outside that door with only a soul cake for defense or hesitating long enough that it broke the door down completely. A second thunderous thud against the door elicited a shriek from her when she fumbled for another of the cakes.

Zebby swung open the door before the possessed animal had enough time to make a third assault. She was not prepared, however, when the large furry body impacted with her instead. Even if she had braced herself, it would not have helped. The bear forcing its way into her home was too big and powerful. The close encounter left Zebby stunned and prone on the floor, vulnerable to the bear's attacks. Fortunately, the soul cake grasped in her hand had spilled to the floor between her and her attacker. When it raised itself onto its hind legs and its front paw lifted in preparation to strike, it saw Zebby's fallen gift and hesitated, sparing its victim for the moment.

Zebby returned to her senses, shaking off her daze, in time to watch the bear inhale the soul cake. With a snuffle and a groan, the bear abandoned its assault, shambling its way out the door instead. Zebby crawled to the door and fought the wind to shut it, groaning herself.

She was sure that bear had been her papa, as mean and as intimidating as ever. He had left her with the usual bruises on her flesh, lump in her throat, and terror in her heart. She was extremely relieved to see him go, but he would not be the last.

Dragging herself painfully from the floor and trying to ignore the taste of blood in her mouth, she hastily sought out the next soul cake. Two were left. Her All Hallow's Eve ordeal would soon be over.

Zebby was grateful she had a few moments reprieve before her next uninvited guest. She drew deep breaths to clear her head and restore her wits, wondering how much she would hurt by morning. At least the deed would be done, and she could focus on atoning for her sins.

Keeping awake proved to be the biggest challenge despite the way her head throbbed, her body ached, and her home rattled in the howling wind. The physical altercations had left her exhausted, countering the stimulant effect of her fear.

The next revenant did not announce itself by scratching at the door but, rather, by offering up a deep, rumbling growl. Had it not been so loud and low to the ground, Zebby might have missed it amongst the pounding of rain and occasional crash of thunder.

The creature behind the door sprang at her the moment she opened it, even though she clutched a soul cake in her free hand. Zebby used that arm to shield her face when the smaller furry body raked at her with lengthy claws, spitting and snarling. *A fisher*, she thought while she tried to thrust the soul cake in its direction. From its meanness, it had to be her brother Mal.

"Go away, Mal," she shrieked, shoving the cake at his snapping mouth. "Just eat the damned soul cake and go away."

Somehow, despite blinded effort, she connected with his mouth, and thankfully, the soul cake proved too tempting. The beast that harboured Mal's vengeful spirit devoured the treat in a single motion. It then ceased any further attacks and retreated into the storm.

It took everything Zebby had left in her to reach out and close the door behind him, struggling against the harsh wind and rain to do so. Once that was done, she lay on the floor, hugging herself and sobbing. Her head spun and blood seeped from the gashes Mal had left behind. She wanted nothing more than the horrible night to be over. It might allow her family's souls to rest, but it would leave her scarred in more ways than one.

But there was still one left. The most innocent amongst them.

Zeke.

Zebby had one soul cake waiting. She dragged herself off the floor, leaving a pinkish trail of rain mixed with blood. She tried to shake off the rain and wipe dry her hands when she picked up her final offering, but her damp fingertips adhered slightly to its floury surface.

The last arrival came more quickly than she expected, but she had lost track of time after her father left her stunned and Mal left her in the mess she was in. They had both been the hardest on her and would have been far more bent on revenge than

Calvin or Clem. But Zeke had been the youngest, with the most to lose, untainted by sin. Zebby had been the closest thing he had to a mother, and it was her fault he had died a horrible, painful death. She couldn't bear to face him, guilt sitting in her stomach like a thorny burr and choking air from her lungs.

When the knock came—and it was just a knock, not a scratching, scraping, or banging—Zebby closed her eyes and held out the last cake when she opened the door. If Zeke chose to maul her before accepting her gift, so be it. She deserved the punishment he would dole out—and far worse.

When the soul cake gently left her hand, the only thing assaulting her was wind and rain. Nothing pounced on her from the doorway, which was entirely unexpected.

"Gee, thanks. I wasn't expecting a welcoming gift. I'm starving."

Because she recognized the voice greeting her as Maynard's, Zebby's eyes joyfully sprang open. Someone had granted her wish from earlier that evening, without having to confess her wrong-doings to the young man. That delight was short-lived, however, when she realized her beau was devouring the last of the soul cake. Glee turned to shock.

"Oh, Maynard, no. That was for Zeke."

"Zeke?" His eyes filled with pity. "Zeke's gone. You need to let him go. Are you bleeding?"

But Zeke wasn't gone. He had come looking for revenge, and the soul cake meant to appease him was no more.

As soon as Zebby heard growling from behind Maynard, she tried stepping back to close the door, tugging on Maynard's arm to pull him along with her. The lanky young man didn't budge, already in the process of turning around to see where the noise had come from and bracing himself protectively to bar the path to Zebby.

Maynard's efforts proved futile. The wolf with glowing red eyes that had come for a specific target launched his way through the human obstacle, bowling over Maynard to clear a path to Zebby.

Knowing she was doomed, Zebby didn't try to run or fight. She crouched and covered her head with her arms, waiting for Zeke's revenge and praying he would spare poor Maynard after he was done with her. Thanks to the loss of the soul cake, no opportunity would exist for atonement.

Waiting for pain and sure death, Zebby hoped Hell wouldn't be as bad as the preacher always claimed.

# GLASS PUZZLE
## Shelly Macaroy

**O**f all the times he had seen Ruby die in his mind, actually seeing his knife's snake-like curves move toward her body—being there during the process of her last breath—trumped each fantasy. He watched her eyelids open wide in horror. Tears he wanted to lick slid down her cheeks. He yanked her mousey hair, feeling her breath against his prickly bearded neck. She pushed. Shoved. Her chest met his knife. Vermilion juices shot from her body and down the blade. She slumped to the ground, her pale skin contrasting with the dark of the grass and soil. Woodland creatures were her only witnesses. She gasped a dying breath. "Why, Darmik?"

He smirked. His knife reunited with her five more times.

She gripped autumn leaves. Her teeth met her lips while the cold of death consumed what was left of her once-warm life.

*** 

**D**armik sat on a barstool in the comedy club. He sipped a reddish drink and focused on the stage while George, a comedian he knew, began his act.

"How are *you* tonight?" George's pronunciation of the word *you* caused patrons to laugh.

One man in the audience yelled, "Fine."

"Fine? Why, that's great. Fantastic. You know, I was driving through one of them burger joints earlier. The cashier asked me the very same question. I'm thinking: What does that have to do with what I wanna put into my belly? *I'm hungry*. That's how I am."

The audience giggled.

"'How am I?' I repeat. 'Yes, sir. How are you today?' he says again—again!" George hesitated for laughs.

"'Now that you asked,'" he glared, "'I'm terrible! A truck hit my family last week. They're all dead. I've been in my house crying for days, and the one thing I thought would take my mind off everything was a burger from this here place. Not just any burger, but a double with cheese and some of that there bacon. But then—then you gotta ask me about my feelings and whatnot instead of my order. Now all I can think about is the truck that killed my family.'

"'Um, I'm sorry,' says my latest victim—I mean the fella. So I says, 'Can I have my damn double cheeseburger with bacon now?'"

The room erupted with laughter.

"Bet that's the last time he asked some pointless question." George paced the stage. Lights gave him a golden glow. "When did these people stop taking orders and start becoming therapists?"

Darmik laughed so loud he gripped his chest.

"Speaking of the service industry, I was at the store looking to make my family some soup for dinner. Yeah, they're not dead; I lied. I needed chicken-flavored bouillon cubes. All I come across is this stuff like 'em. I ask the clerk if it's the same. He gives me a look like I'm the biggest a-hole in the world, followed by saying, 'I don't speak Spanish. You assume 'cause I'm Mexican I can speak the language?' He mutters, 'Racist.'

"I says to him, 'For one, Pablo, bouillon is a French word. And no, I'm not racist. See, over the tag with your name on your shirt it reads, HOW MAY I HELP YOU? I was gullible enough to believe you'd do your damn job.'"

Applause consumed the room.

"Since when is it racist to ask for customer service? I'll tell you the truth of the matter. People are judgy. Judgy and withdrawn with them cell phones and pads. When my son asked me for one of them pads last Christmas, I told him those were for Momma during special times of the month. 'Stay away from her stuff,' I told him."

Darmik snorted into his drink.

"The wife didn't like when I told our son my little joke. She got all judgy. 'You don't say that to a five-year-old.' She's always making judgy comments. 'Wash your hands *before* you eat.'"

George paused while the room settled. "Judginess everywhere! I met the guru of judgy once. I was with a few friends. One of them's here tonight."

Darmik made a cheers motion with his drink.

George waved.

"This musta been ten years ago, folks. We were walkin' through a big ole outside car show. The place had everything. The Lotus. The Skyline. The Lamborghini. The front end of a Dodge attached to the front end of a dadgum Ford." George's eyes moved side to side. A few people cackled.

"The friend here says, 'Now look at her.' My other bud says, 'Way out of our league.' Oh, she's thick in all the right places." George motioned to his rear and chest while pouting his lips to get a few chuckles from the crowd. "Then I note glitter on her face. *Glitter!* Give me a moment to rant." He touched his temples with his thumb and index finger.

"I don't know why women do this. My seven-year-old daughter likes to play with glitter. When she puts the junk on her face, her momma wipes the stuff off and tells her no. But when some young missy in skimpy shorts and a tight shirt wears glitter on purpose, people praise the act. I don't understand. Why on God's green earth would an adult individual decide to play with glitter? It's something kids use to make cute pictures on arts and crafts day, not a makeup accessory!"

Darmik clapped.

George wiped his sweaty forehead. He yanked the microphone off the stand and walked along the stage, laughing with the crowd. "So there I was, starin' at this gal who had glitter on her face. I had to admit she was pretty. Hundreds of people were walking around her. Yet she stood out like a shiny diamond in elephant poo.

"So I says to one friend, 'There's no such thing as a league. Go talk to her, man.' He laughed. My friend here tonight added, 'You go talk to her.' The other said, 'Yeah, bet she won't let you get a word in.'"

George widened his eyes and the crowd whooped. "I walked over to the little lady. 'Excuse me, miss,' my friend said. Before I could get my word in, she shoved her hand in my face. 'I'm not interested.'"

Darmik laughed so loudly people stared, and George winked at him.

"I was put off, but I couldn't let everybody down. 'Excuse me,' my friend said—

"Again with the hand! 'I'm waiting on my boyfriend. Beat it, shortie.'

"I see my friends laughing. I turn back to her, cuff my hands, and yell, 'Can someone please tell this judgy little missy'—I pointed at her—'there's bird shit on her head? I'm trying to tell her there's a wad of white crap in her hair, but she thinks I'm hitting on her. Will someone else try to tell her?' And that judgy priss ran like the roadrunner."

Everyone in the room burst out in laughter. "This story has two morals. Don't be judgy, sure. But most of all—most of all never ever call a short guy—"

"Shortie," the audience said with him in unison.

"That's right. Because we'll either scar your pride or—we'll kill ya." When he smiled with his mouth open and raised his eyebrows, everyone laughed. "Y'all have been great. If you happen to order a double cheeseburger with bacon from the place down the street, tell them you're *feeling hungry*."

George exited the stage.

After the show ended, George approached Darmik. "D-Man."

"Shortie."

Both laughed.

"Great to see you, George. Let me get you a drink."

"Not here. People are going to keep asking me for—"

"Could I have your autograph?"

George signed a woman's napkin as others approached. He wrote his name on a few paper pads fans brought over. "Thank you. Thank you. Thank *you*."

He faced Darmik and whispered, "More to come unless we leave now."

George signed a headshot and handed the picture to a couple. "Have a great night." The pair walked off.

"Let's go to this dive down the road. Best double cheeseburger with bacon you'll have this side of Atlanta," George said.

"Okay, but I'm driving. The least I could do since you agreed to meet."

Darmik and George entered the dive, sat at the bar, and ordered bacon double cheeseburgers.

"That was some thick bacon." Darmik licked ketchup off his thumb. He paid the bartender for two beers and motioned to the pool table in the middle of the room. "Up for a game?"

George wiped tomato juice mixed with grease from his mouth with the paper napkin. "You know this, bud."

They looked at each other as though a decade had not passed. George's once-fit waist hit the table. Darmik racked the pool balls with his shaky hands.

"I hear you're doing well in the guitar bizz." George broke.

"Yep, boy. Building them myself. We sell a ton. No surprise. Guitars sell like—well, cheeseburgers in Los Angeles."

"Whatever happened to playing in a band? Hooking up with ah . . . Ruby?" George missed his second shot. He sipped his beer.

"Women, they're a glass puzzle. You try to help put them together and they cut you for it with their shards of drama."

"A little sexist, don't you think?" George asked. "My wife's nice."

Darmik chuckled. "Yet, you haven't mentioned her name. You settled 'cause you couldn't get Jazz."

George didn't argue.

"Here's what happened," Darmik said. "Ruby told me if I followed her to LA and made something of myself, she'd marry me. That's why I tried to start a band in the first place. I got the guitar, but never the band. I ended up with the business. By the time I was 'successful' by her standards, she'd married someone else. Actually, I heard Ruby went missing the other day. Funny you should bring her up." Darmik hit the cue ball. The nine went into the center pocket. His game was almost perfect until he missed the eight ball.

"Sucks, dude." George hit a solid in. Then another. He made his next shot, but missed one afterward.

Darmik could have won the game. Instead he obviously missed the eight on purpose. "Go ahead. You've got a few hard shots left, and I only have the one. Might as well give you a free hit."

Two of George's solids were in the center of the table. He smacked both balls. They split in the middle and went into separate corner pockets. He moved the pool stick behind his back, aimed at his other ball, and hit it into the far corner. The eight remained on the table. He hooked the ball in for the win. "You could have won."

"You've been practicing." Darmik gave his friend a high five. "That was awesome. Epic, in fact." He sounded eighteen again.

"Well, I do own a pool table. The wife I *settled* for—Jill, by the way—bought it for me on my birthday."

Darmik grimaced. Then he cackled. "A comedian and a hustler!"

The two laughed, and the set of beers became several over the next few hours. They talked and reminisced at the bar.

"Whatever happened to Jazz?"

"Jazz?" George rubbed his drunken face. "I haven't thought about her in years. Man. Talk about a blast from the past. She married some lawyer a while back. Jazz never liked me. You know that."

"But you *loved* her."

George gulped his beer and signaled for another. "Hey now, I wouldn't say love. Strong word. I love Sunday football. I love my kids. I love my little lady at home. There's where I'd use the word." He hiccupped. "I fancied Jazz."

Darmik tilted his head. "Can't believe she pretended to be a lesbian so guys would leave her alone. Always told you she was pretending. And look, she married a dude. Who was right? Who was right? Who was right?" Darmik pushed George's shoulder. "Look—look, who was right?"

"You were right. Happy?"

Darmik sipped beer. "Why, no. You turned down every girl I tried to hook you up with back when we were kids, even the one I locked you in a room with. Some of them were pretty hot. You said you were waiting for Jazz. You compared how much you 'fancied' her to how much I loved Ruby. Only, I was with her. Ruby was honest with me. She said if I got my shit straight, I could come find her in LA and sweep her off her feet. Just she didn't want to wait forever. Jazz *always* lied to you. Don't know how you moved on."

George's bloodshot eyes squinted. He shook his head. "That's the point. I moved on. Sure, she broke my heart and didn't even take notice. The only time she paid attention to me was when she needed something. Then Jazz married a guy even though she always claimed to be gay. So what! Life worked out for me. I have a family. I'm happy. Jazz never liked me. So what! The lies are on her conscience, not mine."

"But, dude, you were a virgin how long because you waited for her? How long did you pause your love life for her?"

George squeezed a fist. His left eyelid flinched. "You already know."

Darmik slicked his fading hair. "College! I mean, what were you? Twenty-two, twenty-three?"

"Drop it. Please."

"Please, please, please. There's your problem, George, always pleasing when you should take action. Jazz would have been with you if you weren't so damn *nice* to her. Do something for once in your life."

"What do you mean? What should I do?"

"Get revenge." Darmik's eye gleamed.

"This is starting to sound weird." George stood.

"Wait, buddy. I'm not talking about anything sadistic, just some old school fun. Make us remember them good ole days. Principal Peters' style."

"We're thirty. I'm not egging some old crush's house at"—he looked at his wrist—"something-o'clock in the morning."

31

Darmik dropped cash on the table. "The bar's closing and we need something to do, so why not? You owe it to yourself. For the good ole days, dude."

George shook his head. "I should . . . I should get home."

"I came all this way." Darmik lowered his head as if in defeat.

George rubbed his forehead. "Even if I agreed, I don't want to go into some store, drunk as I am, and buy eggs and toilet paper. They call what you want to do vandalism. Plus, I don't have a clue where she lives. What if she doesn't even live in Atlanta anymore?"

Darmik presented a piece of paper with an address. "Eggs and TP are in my car, dude."

They left the bar, and Darmik drove to a secluded house. Off to the side were a red shed and a private pond with ducks.

George grabbed the eggs.

Darmik got out of his car and handed George the toilet paper. "Hold this a second. Before we start, I have a surprise for you." He entered the shed and exited minutes later, dragging a gagged and tied-up woman. He grinned deviously.

The woman, wearing bloodstained clothing, appeared scared and shaken. Purple bruises were visible despite the dried blood that lined her face and arms. She seemed to lack the strength to fight, and based on her lack of defiance to walk, she was about to collapse. Sheer terror was branded in her stare.

"What the duck?" George dropped the toilet paper and eggs. Yolk glided along the driveway and oozed into the grass nearby where his old crush stood. Her skin was ghost white. Raven black bangs covered her wet cheeks. She yelped in pain. Her wrists were chafed from being tied together, and her legs had slash marks up and down.

Darmik removed the gag with his knife and lowered the blade close to Jazz's long neck. He kicked the back of her knees, and she crashed to the ground.

"This is insane. Untie her!"

"He—he killed my husband!" She squinted. "*George*? Is that—is that you? Help me. Please!"

"Always asking him for favors. Never giving back." Darmik kicked her again, and she fell to her side. "Selfish, cold bitch!"

"*Jazz*! Darmik, whatever sick game you've been playing, it's over." George spread his hands.

"I see you're sober now. I've never had to fake drunk for so long before." Darmik twisted his neck to pop his joints. "You're a lightweight now, shortie."

"Okay, you called me shortie. You win at life because you're tall. Let her go."

"Don't you get it? This is for you." Darmik presented the handle of his knife to George. "I ended Ruby. Now you get to do the same to Jazz. Then we'll be together."

"What?"

"No homo. I mean we'll share a bond like no one else. We'll be friends forever."

"We were friends—*were* being past tense." George swatted the knife from Darmik's hand and in the same step punched him in the eye.

Darmik fell to the ground and rolled to his stomach. Using his palms, he pushed himself up and breathed deeply.

George picked up a rock.

*Whack!*

George lifted the snake-shaped knife.

"I—I—I can't believe Darmik tried to kill me," Jazz mumbled.

"*Tried*?" George said. "Who says he didn't succeed?"

Jazz emitted a loud, short-lived scream.

# URSULA
## L.S. Engler

I'm sorry, Mister Fontaine," Dr. Ilsa Davenport said, closing the file, "Ursula Navidson is no longer a *resident* here at Oak Ridge." She placed her hand on the file like one would set down a paperweight as if she thought I would snatch the documents. But I just sat there, stiff and cold in my chair on the other side of her desk.

Her hesitation on the word *resident* rang in my head like a misshapen bell, a small fumble in an otherwise precise speech. I eyed the dark brown file underneath her hand, pondering its secrets, but I had a hunch nothing helpful would be inside. This was a dummy file, the one that made them look good, as if everything was perfectly normal, everything in order. Inside was the dossier with the basics: name, date of birth, parents, spouse, children, hair color, eye color, weight, height, blah blah blah. A photograph of Ursula in better times, classically beautiful, tragically so, her soft blonde hair a halo around her cherubic face. Another photograph of Ursula in recent times, still beautiful but haunted, wild and feral, her hair a nest, and those eyes that could cut straight to the hard, bitter truth, as sharp and cold as a knife. Dull reports: check-ups, check-ins, therapy, and medications. Contacts in case of emergency—my name possibly, a longshot at the bottom, right under Tanya from work or the childhood neighbor who sometimes watched her when she was a kid.

But I didn't want to see any of that. I wanted to see what was probably buried in a basement no one knew about: real notes, real ledgers, experiments that would never see the light of day. I would find Ursula there in their darkest secrets, nowhere near the bright neatness of Davenport's quiet office.

I forced a congenial smile, straining against my anger. "I understand. I wouldn't have expected her to recover so quickly, but that's great news. Can I ask where she's gone? Did she go back home? A half-way house, maybe? Somewhere else?"

Davenport's mouth puckered for a moment. She regarded me with an accusing glint in her eyes, but she swept it away as quick as a blink with a sudden burst of an apologetic smile. "I'm so sorry, Mister Fontaine, but that information is classified."

"Yes." I chuckled lightly. Oh silly, foolish me! "Yes, of course. Can't just disclose that sort of thing to just anyone who waltzes into your office. But I'm hardly just anyone. Ursula is one of my closest friends. We grew up together, back in Indiana. We sat next to each other in tenth grade chem. We were in the same college prep classes, on the same bus route."

I had hoped these anecdotes would spark recognition, but her demeanor dropped about twenty degrees instead. "I don't recall her ever mentioning you, Mister Fontaine."

I was struck with an urge to swipe that file from underneath her hand and shout *Liar! Liar! Liar!* The idea that Ursula had never mentioned me was impossible after everything she and I had been through. Davenport knew exactly who I was, and that was why she was so cagey. I was angered at her bold-faced falsehoods, but a small voice whispered in my ear, reminding me to calm down, to hold back, to tread lightly. Ursula could have kept things quiet to protect me, graciously leaving me out of whatever nefarious schemes had entrapped her behind the heavy mahogany doors of Oak Ridge Institute.

"Ursula has received the necessary tools to reach out to her friends and family if she desires." Davenport spoke with an infuriating calmness. "When she's ready."

"You can't just give me a phone number, an address?" I tried my most charming smile, the last thing left in my arsenal. "Maybe

I could leave something for her and you could pass it along? So she at least knows I was here?"

Davenport held firm. "No, I'm sorry, Mister Fontaine, we can't do that. It wouldn't be appropriate. It's important for her to take her time without any additional *distractions*."

The woman was infuriatingly stubborn. I briefly considered the idea of a bribe, but no, I didn't want trouble. But I wasn't ready to give up, either. I simply had to figure out a different tactic. If Davenport didn't care to cooperate with me on a professional level, that left me no choice but to pursue something more extreme.

"That's fair," I sighed, pushing back my chair and standing. I gave one more cursory scan of the room, hoping to discern anything that might hint at Ursula's fate, but there was nothing. "Thank you for your time, anyway. I'm glad Ursula was well enough to go home, but it sucks that I just missed her."

"I'm sure she would have appreciated your visit, Mister Fontaine," Davenport said, rising from her own seat. "I'll see you out."

My objection was met with the claim that she was headed that way anyway, so I couldn't shake her. With Davenport at my side, it was impossible to sneak off and explore. She spoke dryly of the institution and its method while we walked, mostly to keep up conversation and distract me from the occasional moans and screams coming from the wards upstairs. I didn't pay attention to her in the slightest, instead inspecting the place for weakness and hiding spots, already planning my break-in. Nurses and orderlies passed by, sometimes with patients, and I considered their potential danger. They also made for a good study, so I noted their dispositions in order to copy them and blend in.

My attention lingered for a moment on a frail slip of a woman draped in a white hospital gown. A burly nurse, gripping the patient, led her past us, keeping her close to the wall. Davenport stiffened slightly at my side, a subtle change but enough for me to notice. Anyone that would make Davenport nervous was someone I needed to learn more about.

The tiny woman in the large gown giggled, but she stopped suddenly as if someone had slapped her or spoken a harsh word.

Her eyes widened, head jerking while she tried to find the source of the insult, and then her tittering laughter resumed as if nothing had happened.

"You!" The moment the patient saw me, she stopped and shouted, trying to point despite being restrained. Her knees buckled, and the nurse struggled to keep her up. She squirmed, but her eyes never left me. "It's you! You're him. She said you would save us." Her giggles turned manic. "Don't listen to them. Don't listen! They're liars, all of them. You have to save us. You have to save her!"

"Susanna!" Davenport's sharp voice cut off the wild claims. She held out an arm to stop me from moving forward as if to protect me. "That's enough! Whoever you think this is I can assure you that you are mistaken. Besides, that is not how we converse with other people, is it? I will kindly ask you to stop all this ranting and apologize to Mister Fontaine."

"Fontaine. That's right!" Susanna's face brightened with childlike glee. "That's what she said. Fontaine will save her! Fontaine will save us! Save us, Fontaine, our Savior!" Her shrill laughter filled the hall.

No matter how much I wanted to believe her words, I had to doubt Susanna's sanity. Had she known Ursula? Did she really recognize my name, or was she merely parroting what she'd heard?

"Apologies, sir," the nurse muttered. "She gets so excited. Come on, Susanna, we can't bother our visitors. Say goodbye. You're going to be late for your meeting with the doctor." She pulled Susanna toward another hallway that branched away from us.

A dreamy look passed over the patient's face, the wildness dropping away. Her head lolled back when she smiled at me. "Bye-bye," she cooed. "Bye-bye, Fontaine. Nick Fontaine. We'll see each other again soon."

She winked, or twitched, or something, right before she turned. I was rooted to the spot. I had never seen this woman previously, and she could have mimicked my last name from Davenport, but where had she picked up my first name? It could hardly have been a lucky guess. What else did Susanna know?

I couldn't tell you how long I gawked after this mysterious woman, but Susanna and her nurse were long gone by the time Davenport pulled me back to the moment.

"Mister Fontaine, I think it's best you get going."

"Yes," I agreed, reluctant to turn, but I did, hoping to pass off my dazed disposition as simply being shocked by the absurdity of it all. "Yes, I suppose it is."

***

**M**y body may have left Oak Ridge that afternoon, but my mind remained, lingering in the hallways trying to reveal their secrets. I allowed myself to imagine there was no duplicity and that Ursula had been released and was starting over happily in a nice little condo nearby, where they could keep an eye on her and be there for any relapses in whatever mental condition they claimed she had. I scoured the local telephone books, the library, the Internet for her name, an address—any sign of her at all. I scouted out buildings recently sold or for rent in the area, pouring over real estate listings and property management documents to discern anything that might appear to be owned by the institute or any of their affiliates. I even tried to look up Susanna, finding several dozen leads before I happened on a newspaper article that gave me her full story.

Five years ago, one Susanna Hendricks went crazy and killed her baby half-brother and her mother in their sleep. I couldn't imagine that frail thing capable of such an act, but that was definitely her in the grainy newsprint picture, chin lifted defiantly toward the camera as if she regretted nothing.

Doubt flooded me then, causing me to second guess myself. If Susanna was at Oak Ridge instead of a prison, then she was justifiably insane, rehabilitation more beneficial than incarceration. Had I been swayed by the rantings of a madwoman? I kept coming back to my name, *Nick Fontaine*, on Susanna's lips, remembering the twitching curl in the corner of her mouth.

I had to persevere. My investigations were coming up dry. I had no proof, only a feeling, so I had to get inside Oak Ridge, deep into the bowels of where they hid the secret of whatever they had done with the love of my life. It might be the desperate measures of a man with nothing to lose, but at least it was something.

Two weeks after my first inquiry about Ursula, two weeks later than I would have liked, I decided everything was too clean, too well hidden. I prepared to infiltrate the institute and find out what happened to my Ursula.

I decided to make my move on Wednesday morning. Any excitement from the weekend would have calmed, all the orderly tasks of Monday and the catch-up of Tuesday out of the way. Anticipation for the following weekend wouldn't have begun, and night time, while less populated, was more carefully monitored. The overnight shift would be on the way out; the day shift would be settling in, the patients sedate with breakfast in their bellies and pills under their tongues. If everything went as planned, I could walk in and find what I needed right under their noses.

The clincher would be acting like I belonged, that I had been there the whole time, even if no one particularly noticed or remembered me. I would be questioned at the main entrance, so I waited by the maintenance shed until I had the chance to slip a key card from a worker's lanyard while he gathered what he needed for the day. I hoped I'd be gone before he realized it was missing.

Once I had the key card, I headed for the side door of the main building and searched for an orderly's uniform and a clipboard, the classic elements of a break-in disguise. With enough confidence, no one would look at me twice.

I terrorized the halls of Oak Ridge as if I were a ghost possessed, muttering about charts and projections until I found the stairwell. I earned a few curious glances, but the halls were mostly empty. Even bumps and other noises from above seemed muted and subdued in the quiet late-morning sunlight.

I descended the stairs to the basement, which my research told me would be a labyrinthian mess of hallways and offices, examination rooms and storage space. Oak Ridge consisted of four main buildings, although one was rarely used, and an underground network of corridors connected them to make things easier for the staff. In the underworld, they would run their tests and perform physical training, where they'd keep particularly loud patients and underpaid undergrad students. None of these interested me; I merely wanted to find my way to the south building, the mostly unused one, where they were sure to hold their private documents *and* people.

At least the place was brightly lit, with smooth clean walls and bold plastic placards with directions and maps. This was a state-of-the-art medical facility, not a dreary asylum from a gothic novel. I found my way around easily, checking the occasional door to see if it might reveal my Ursula or any indication of her. I was about to slip up the stairwell to the south building when the sounds of measured footsteps and voices stopped me. I couldn't make out the words, but I recognized one of the voices as Doctor Ilsa Davenport's.

If she saw me, she would recognize me immediately, but this could possibly be my best chance to discover where they'd hidden Ursula. I moved my hand away from the door, slinking back against the wall while I moved toward the sound of Davenport's voice. Was she coming or going? I prayed for the latter, imagining myself trailing after her and drinking up every word from within the shadows.

"We'll have to proceed with caution," Davenport said. There was more I couldn't hear. Then they walked away, and I crept forward enough to see two people turning the far corner. I scurried after them with soft feet and a held breath, clipboard on the ready if anyone appeared from a door or side corridor and questioned me.

"Let's increase the medication intake," Davenport said, "but not too much. We're not getting the results we want, but I don't want to hurt the poor thing, either." She rambled off a long string of medical babble, the young woman beside her scribbling, obviously terrified of getting even one little detail wrong. The more Davenport spoke, the more my blood boiled. I had no idea what any of it meant, but I was sure it involved Ursula. It took everything I had not to turn that next corner at full speed, pouncing on the doctor and holding her hostage until they set her free from their mad machinations.

I almost did, too. The woman with Davenport whispered. I couldn't hear her words and prepared for a drastic but necessary step. But then the quiet murmuring stopped, punctuated with a surprised sound from Davenport.

"Mister Anderson," she said. "I was just on my way to see you. We need to have a word about the security of the place lately."

The unseen Mr. Anderson scoffed, a sound suggesting burliness. The voice that followed matched, and I regretted not having a weapon since the clipboard would hardly suffice. "That's what I came to see you about, doctor. Hendley in maintenance reported his missing badge, and I'd like permission to search the wards in case a patient has it. I also took the liberty of sending a few men out on a grounds sweep already."

My heartbeat became a loud, deep thrumming in my ears, so loud I thought it might echo in the underground corridors. I wouldn't have much time, and most of my potential escape routes would be infiltrated by now.

"Yes, of course," Davenport said. "Thank you. You remember that Fontaine fellow I told you about? This has him written all over it. Keep a close eye out. I want the authorities involved if he's anywhere near Oak Ridge."

My throat went dry and my heart dropped to my shoes, but I couldn't help a small, preening twinge deep in my stomach. Davenport knew I was a threat, and she was afraid of something. It only bolstered my certainty that she hid something big. But if I didn't find Ursula soon, I might never find her. I had already given Davenport enough to detain me for good, and I'd be no help to Ursula if I was stuck behind bars—or worse.

I wanted to follow Davenport and the other woman, but it was too risky. Anderson could be heading my way, and the basement had far too many twists and turns. Three doors were at my disposal in my current location. One of them, with a little plaque that read STASIS LAB, was locked. The one beside it, labeled STASIS ROOM, was not, and the third, on the opposite side, was unlocked, too, and appeared to be a storage closet. An excellent place to hide, but a terrible place to find my Ursula. I ducked into the Stasis Room, closing the door behind me, but there was no lock. Damn.

And I was not alone, either. I turned to find a woman in a white jacket staring at me and a familiar woman perched on a table at the center of the room. Susanna. Her face was white with surprise, and her jaw dropped almost comically. A jolt of panic raced through me. Would Susanna help me? Or would her wildness give me away? I had to think quickly, but my mind felt too scrambled to be effective.

"May I help you?" the woman in the coat asked. Her voice was a bit barbed, irritated by the interruption. "Lost your way, sir?"

I opened my mouth, but nothing came out, so I shook my head while I grasped for something, anything, to help me. "Stop," I choked out and realized how desperate and strangled I sounded. I cleared my throat and tried again, straightening my shoulders to convey a sense of authority, even if it felt like a ridiculous caricature that no one would ever actually believe. "We need you to stop Susanna's procedure"—whatever that may have been—"immediately. I need to return her to her room straight away."

Even when the words left me, I knew they were too hollow. The irritation on the doctor's face deepened when I had been hoping confusion would take its place. "They would have called me," she said. "There's no way you could have made it down here before a phone call."

"It really is urgent," I babbled, mostly filling the space while my brain tried to catch up. "They couldn't call. An unknown individual has gained access to the facility and—"

Before I could finish, Susanna rose to the occasion. She grabbed the metal tray from the rolling cart beside the examination table. The tools and syringes rained down on the tile floor, and before the doctor could turn, Susanna crashed the tray into the other woman's face. The dull, resonating sound wasn't enough to knock her out. I realized too late that Susanna's attempt to save us wasn't going to work. Her eyes implored me, begging, pleading, but all I could do was gurgle. The doctor, her face red from anger and the impact of the tray, pulled a Taser from her belt and jammed it into Susanna's neck.

I didn't stick around to see Susanna collapse to the floor and convulse. I rushed from the room before the doctor turned her self-defence mechanisms on me. She would be on the phone in a heartbeat, alerting security to my presence, requesting help with the insurgent Susanna, and more than likely, the place would be on lockdown. Doors would be sealed, guards posted, and surveillance increased until the madman on the loose was caught. I was trapped, with nowhere to turn, nowhere to run, and no idea where to find Ursula.

Dread and hopelessness weighed down my feet, but I still ran as quickly as I could, trying to recall the maps I'd seen, trying to figure out where I could go, where they might be hiding Ursula. Perhaps I could still find her and, together, we could work out a solution and escape. She'd been here for the past five years; surely, she'd have picked up some ideas, clever as she was. Maybe the key was to let the whole thing blow over. Find a breakroom and pretend I'd been on my lunch break the whole time.

Yeah, right. The only people who would believe that story were the crazy ones here as patients. In addition to that, I'd managed to get horribly lost in my desire to flee. None of the doors or plaques were familiar; even the color of the walls had changed, a pale putrid green instead of the previous honey yellow. I must have taken a turn toward the basement under another building. My heart surged when I thought I was being led straight to Ursula, by some strange magnetic connection, by serendipity, by fate. It almost felt as though she called to me, guided me, told me where to go. Still, any supernatural assistance from her was weak at best—and breathless, I slowed long enough to gawk at another map on the wall. My excitement blurred my vision, making it difficult to read, but I bulged my eyes and blinked, clearing away the mist so I could find out where I was and proceed with certainty and confidence.

One word cleared: southern. And a voice echoed through the hallway and turned my blood cold.

"There he is. Get ready."

Davenport. She stood at the end of the hallway with two burly guards flanking her, their guns pointed and ready. "Mister

Fontaine," she said, her voice firm like a brick wall, "we can do this the easy way or the hard way. It's really up to you. You've violated a truckload of laws with this little stunt, but maybe we can turn a blind eye to most of them if you cooperate and come with me. We don't need to stir up any more trouble."

"Just tell me where Ursula is," I demanded, bolstering myself as if I had an arsenal of weapons at my disposal though all I had was confidence and fury. "That's all I want. Just tell me where she is, and I'll be on my way."

"You know I can't do that, Nick." She dropped the dramatics, maybe in an attempt to lower my guard, but it only made me raise my defences. This woman manipulated minds professionally. I couldn't let her sway me. "One more chance. Step down, or else you'll leave us no choice but to detain you."

My fists clenched so tightly at my sides that I thought my knuckles might burst. The veins in my neck popped out in sharp relief. "Where is she?" My voice boomed, forced out by the tight pressure in my chest.

Everything happened quickly after that. I forced myself to move, a howl tearing out of me when I barreled toward them, uncertain what I would do once I got there. Davenport backed away and shouted her order. The first bullet got me in the leg, causing me to stagger. The next one hit me in my shoulder; it might have pierced my heart if the first shot hadn't pitched my body forward into a new position. The second bullet pulled me back, and I fell to the floor, hissing in pain. Just when my fingers found the hot blood soaking into my jacket, a dart pierced my neck. A pinprick, but that was all it took to send a tingling heat through me. Blackness crowded my vision before it completely took over.

**W**hen I woke up from fitful forced slumber, my first sensation was a powerfully dry mouth that made me smack my lips and tongue in a futile effort to coax out saliva. That was when I realized I lay on a thin vinyl-covered mattress on a stark metal spring bed. Pain seeped into my consciousness from my thigh and shoulder, and I groaned when I remembered the two hits I'd taken. I sounded like a pathetic, lowing cow while I writhed from pain that intensified by the second. The wounds had been patched while I was out, but they still hurt, dull aches that made reality all the more horrific.

The room was tiny and barren, with a twin bed, a small table, a chest of drawers, and a sink. Harsh afternoon light filled the small barred window set high on the wall. Another barred window was set into the door, over a little panel in the middle, a place to pass in trays of food and cups of pills. I had been in a room like this before, the soul-crushing cell of an Oak Ridge patient.

Despite the pain, I stood and limped to the door. I grasped the bars. I couldn't see anyone, but I heard voices in the hallway, low as if keeping secrets.

I spoke loudly enough to rise over their murmurings. "Hey, let me out of here! Let me out."

I shook the unmovable bars, hoping to create a scene, although I knew no amount of pleading or begging or shouting would save me. The conversation ceased, and steady footsteps approached, the measured clicking of a woman's heels. I knew it was Davenport before she stepped to the window, chin lifted, held up by a triumphant air.

"Mister Fontaine," she said, "I suggest you calm yourself or else we will have to administer another tranquilizer. However, we won't keep you unlawfully detained. Now that you're awake, we'll contact your lawyer to discuss the matter, but I wouldn't hold your breath. Between breaking and entering, theft of property, and assaulting one of my doctors, we have a very strong case against you without even bringing your restraining order regarding Ursula Navidso—"

"Where is she?" I broke in before she could complete that nonsense statement, another lie in her wheelhouse of manipulation. "What have you done with her? I will find her. You know I will. If you think some shots and tranqs and steel bars will hold me back, then I'm afraid you're the crazy one here, not me. You can try to hide her all you want, but I will find her."

Worn and weary, Davenport sighed, a woman who had gone over this many times. "You won't be going anywhere, Mister

Fontaine, and you will not be going anywhere near her, not on my watch. With all we've done to get her over the trauma of what you've put her through, do you think we would just hand over that information because you asked? A common definition of insanity indicates doing the same thing over and over and expecting a different result, despite evidence to the contrary. You need help, Mister Fontaine, and we can provide that help for you."

"I don't need help," I said, as firmly and calmly as I could muster, though I wanted to break down the door between us. "I need Ursula. You took her from me, and I will get her back."

"We didn't take her from you, Nick. The law did. The law and the restraining order that she herself requested after you—"

"Liar! Liar, liar, liar! She would never do that to me! Never!"

Davenport breathed deeply. "We'll contact your lawyer, Mister Fontaine, but rest assured if you're not staying here under our careful watch, then you'll be locked away somewhere else instead. For your sake, I hope it's with us. We only want to help you."

"You can't keep her away from me!" I shrieked, my face against the bars to watch her walk away. "Just you wait! I will find her! I will. Just you wait."

# HOUSE CALL
## S.D. Hintz

**M**el, the mailman, waved when he slowed to a halt at the end of Robert Curry's driveway. He drove a rust bucket of a mail truck—one of those older models that looked more like a jeep—the best the town of Twin Lakes could provide.

"Mornin', Bob. How goes the battle?"

"Grueling. Finally buckled down on the yard work."

"It's 'bout time. I bet underneath all those dandelions is a little Kentucky bluegrass."

"Or more dandelions. I'd be more than happy to park the damn lawnmower."

Mel chuckled as he pushed up his bifocals and sorted through a handful of mail. "Let's see what I have for you today. Bills . . . Domino's coupons . . . Visa offer . . . the usual."

Bob grabbed the stack. His biggest pet peeve was when Mel studied the stash as if he were a private investigator. But Bob supposed Mel did that with everyone's mail. How could he not, drowning in temptation with a truckload of private information?

Bob rifled through the mail. He picked out a handwritten envelope and studied it. His brows knitted. No return address. Simply his name and location in cursive red ink.

Mel flashed a toothless grin. "Don't go breakin' a sweat now."

Bob forced a smile. "You, either. Thanks, Mel. Have a good one."

He turned and walked up the drive while the truck clunked down the street. He continued to stare at the small envelope.

Chances were good it was junk mail from a real estate agency or roofing company. He failed to recall the last time anyone sent him a letter—or a holiday card, for that matter.

He sat on the front steps and opened the envelope. Inside was a folded piece of crumpled paper torn from a spiral notebook.

Bob was getting more confused by the second. Maybe an elementary student had mistaken him for a pen pal. Or a frat boy had mailed a kegger invitation to the wrong address.

He unfolded the paper, the wrinkles crunching like trodden gravel. One phrase was scrawled with black permanent marker in capital letters: I'M IN YOUR HOUSE.

He glared at the sloppy handwriting. He couldn't take his eyes off the unpunctuated sentence. A flurry of thoughts and accusations bogged his brain.

*What the hell is this? A joke? I bet it's that teenager on the corner. She looks like one of those goth-a-go-go girls with her black eyeliner and fifty ear piercings. That bitch better not even start harassing me. I'll have her in juvey before she can spell "tattoo."*

Bob quickly made up his mind. Ninety-nine percent of the neighborhood had consisted of retirees until the previous month when that single mother and her daughter moved in. It was obvious the Marilyn Manson groupie was bored out of her mind and sending hate mail to her neighbors.

*I wonder if Clara or Herb got one.*

"Hey, Bob!"

Bob jumped and looked up from the paper. His next-door neighbor Herb stood by his garage, smoking a pipe as the breeze tousled his off-white hair. Just the man he wanted to talk to.

"Hey, Herb."

"What you got there? A love note?"

Bob crossed the yard and handed over the paper. "You could say that. It's from that pagan bitch down the street."

Herb's brows arched like rainbows when he grabbed the note. He studied it, and then returned it, taking a life-shortening drag of tobacco.

Bob stared at his friend, expecting a reply. "So? What do you think?"

Herb exhaled as he gazed down the street toward the goth girl's house. "I think you need to see who's in your house."

"Nobody's in my house. I've been out front all morning."

"Is your back door unlocked?"

"My gun cabinet's gonna be unlocked in a minute! There's nobody running around my house! That bitch down the street is playing pranks." Bob huffed, the note trembling in his hand. He shook his head. "Did you check *your* mail yet? I want to know if that bitch singled me out."

Herb exhaled a plume of smoke. "Nah, the flag's still up. Mel's pissed at me. I told him yesterday he should go postal on his wife for gaining fifty pounds."

"You think Clara got one?"

"I doubt it. Her flag's still up, too. Besides, how could somebody be inside two houses at once?"

"No one's in my house!"

"Well, you've got to go in sometime. Won't you be surprised if you walk in and the TV's gone? Not sure why a burglar would mail you a letter to give himself away, though."

Bob's temper boiled. Herb's theories angered him even more. "Why don't you think that little bitch is behind this?"

"What's she ever done to you?"

"Nothing, until now. Except for the Evil Eye."

"She winked at you. Great."

"Fine! I'll go look inside, but I'm telling you, if there's no one in there I'm gonna whoop some ass."

Herb chuckled.

Bob disappeared into the garage.

*I'm in your house . . .*

The note haunted Bob to no end. He simmered at the thought that someone was taunting him. What had he done to piss that bitch off? He had yet to even utter a word to her.

He kicked off his shoes in the entryway and scanned the stairwells of the split-level. The basement was a dim silence. Sunlight poured into the upstairs living room, capturing the dust particles.

A creak. It sounded like a floorboard.

*I'm in your house . . .*

49

Bob shook off the thought. *It's just the house settling, you old fool.*

He took the steps by twos as if charging into battle. His eyes darted like heat-seeking missiles.

The living room.

Empty.

The kitchen.

Dirty, but deserted.

Bob marched down the hall and peered into the bathroom and master bedroom.

No one was in his house.

The doorbell chimed, startling Bob so badly he thought would have a heart attack.

"Goddamn it, Herb!"

He headed downstairs to the entryway, cursing his friend the entire flight. Herb probably wanted to know if the place had been burglarized. He often housesat when Bob was on vacation and no doubt was acting the concerned neighbor. Bob was eager to tell him he was dead wrong and everything was undisturbed.

The doorbell chimed impatiently.

Bob flung open the door. His eyes widened. He felt his face redden and a vein pop in his forehead as his heart gave a roundhouse to his ribcage.

The goth bitch stood before him, waving a clipboard like a fan.

Bob scowled, looking her up and down. He hated her, and he had never met her. Everything about her was shaded in black. Her hair, her lipstick and eyeliner, her studded jeans and matching suspender top, her skull choker and belt buckle—all suffocating her pale, frail frame. He was speechless, a million accusations flying through his head. He was relieved she spoke first.

Her voice was monotone, no nonsense, mature for a schoolgirl. "My mom wants to know if you'll sign a petition. She lives over there on the corner."

Bob's brain ranted. *Petition my ass. You just want another reason to harass me.*

"Petition for what? Little schoolgirls that dress like hookers?"

The girl's pierced brows knitted and her ringed lip curled. "It's for my mom, you fucking asshole. In case you haven't noticed, our mailman is prejudiced."

"What the hell are you talking about? You've lived here a couple of weeks and you're the Neighborhood Watch?"

The girl shook her head and gritted her teeth. "My mom said you would act this way. Look around, you old fuck! You're the only one getting mail!"

His temper exploded. The goth bitch had gone too far. First the prank note and now a petition against Mel. Who the hell did she think she was fooling? She needed a crash course on respecting her elders.

Bob seized her bony arm and yanked her into the house. She stumbled forward, collided with the coat rack, and tumbled to the floor. The clipboard slid and banged against the wall. He slammed the front door and whipped out the crumpled note, waving it in her face. "You put this in my mailbox! Admit it! And now you want to petition Mel out of the neighborhood? You got another thing coming, bitch."

The goth girl's startled look was immediately replaced with repressed rage. She smeared blood, courtesy of a coat hook, that trickled down her cheek. Her pierced lip curled. "You old fuck."

She snatched the note from him, fisted it, and punched him in the groin. He groaned and doubled over. She stood and threw a second jab, shattering his nose. Blood spurted on the front door and dripped on the linoleum.

Bob, one hand on his nuts and the other on his nostrils, staggered back into the wall. "Goddamn whore!"

The goth chick grabbed his ear and tugged him forward so they were face to face. "Now you're gonna sign this petition, grandpa! Or I'm gonna start breaking knuckles! Got it?"

Bob knew his face was blood red. It had been a long time since he wanted to kill somebody, and it had been an even longer time since someone made him bleed. A good fifty years ago when he was fifteen, the high school bully—who looked like a James Dean tattooed drag queen—had slammed the locker door in his face. Rather than collapsing, he had grabbed his X-Acto knife off his science book and flailed it. He slashed the bully's throat and then proceeded to turn him into a pincushion. Two years in juvey made him a better man.

Until now.

Bob reached up and grasped the goth chick's lip ring. He then jerked his arm as hard as he could. Her head and body snapped to the side. Her bottom lip tore off, and she tumbled down the stairwell to the basement, face first on a drumroll of steps.

He gazed down into the shadows, the ringed pink flesh dripping between his fingers like a thawed pork loin. The girl's body twitched at the bottom of the stairs. She moaned, and then rasped a curse.

*I'm in your house . . .*

*That's right*, Bob thought, tossing the flesh aside. It slapped against the wall and splatted on the floor. *You're in my house. And I'll be damned if you're getting out.*

He snatched the discarded clipboard and stomped down the stairs, each *thump* more impending than the last. He crouched beside the girl. She looked up, pierced brows knitted and hate in her eyes. Her top lip quivered uncontrollably.

Bob grinned wickedly, waving the clipboard. "You forgot your petition."

He cracked her on the skull and snapped the clipboard in half. He tossed the remnants into the corner and seized her pierced eyebrow. She moaned, but it rose to a scream when he jerked the ring. Her brow tore in half, spraying blood, and her eyes rolled back.

Bob wasn't satisfied. He yanked her five earrings. Half her right ear separated, and he stuffed it in her mouth. She gagged and moments later shook the death rattle.

He reached behind him and flipped the light switch.

"Hallelujah, Bob, I'm thinkin' we're on the same wavelength."

He whirled to see Mel standing at the other end of the basement. The mailman held a utility knife in one gloved hand and a piece of paper in the other.

Bob narrowed his eyes and wiped his bloody hands on his pants. "Why the hell are you down here, Mel?"

Mel pushed up his bifocals. "I'd ask you the same, but it's pretty obvious." He waved the piece of paper. "Forgot to put the second note, sayin' 'I'm in your basement,' on your back door. I was hopin' you saw my truck parked." He pointed the knife at the rectangular window.

Bob stepped and squinted. Sure enough, the rust bucket was parked two houses down. Not only that, every mailbox down the street had its flag up. His victim's deadpan voice rang in his head: *Look around, you old fuck! You're the only one getting mail!*

He looked back at Mel. "What is this? You're in my house . . . and I'm the only one getting mail?"

"Well, look at your neighbors. They're crazy. You're the only one who hasn't been actin' a fuckin' prick."

Bob ran his hands through his hair. "Christ, what have I done? I thought that bitch was in my house. Goddamn it, Mel. Why didn't you put your name on the note?"

"Wouldn't have mattered. You would've killed that bitch at some point."

"That's right! I killed her, Mel. Over a goddamn note you wrote! And some stupid petition!"

Mel removed his glasses and hooked them on his uniform pocket. "That's no petition. She saw me goin' in your house. Probably thought you were takin' sides."

*"What?"*

Mel pointed the knife at the dead girl. "You didn't notice her ankle? She's on house arrest."

Bob turned and eyed her. Below a tattoo of a skeletal snake was a black ankle bracelet with a blinking red light. His mind scattered. "If she's on house arrest—"

Mel plunged the knife into a rectangular box, and Bob suddenly took notice of the surroundings. Two cardboard coffins constructed out of post office boxes lay at Mel's feet. How long had Mel been sneaking into his house, especially since Bob rarely went in the basement?

Mel glared at the goth girl's lifeless body and spat, "She killed my retriever, Bob. Snapped Goldy's neck for barkin'. Judge put her on house arrest for a year, ordered her to relocate twenty miles out. Well, wouldn't you know the bitch ended up on my route? Saw her name on an envelope one day and knew right there she had it comin'."

Bob backpedaled slowly. His heel nudged the dead body. "Mel, if she's on house arrest, the cops are gonna be here any second."

"Ain't that the truth. And you got the only mailbox with the flag down. Bit of a *red flag*, wouldn't you say?"

"Goddamn it, Mel, what're we gonna do?"

"*We? Your* fingerprints are all over her." Mel pulled his knife out of the cardboard and gestured. "You got no choice but to put her in a box."

Bob's rage increased, and he felt his face flush. He wanted nothing more than to throttle Mel. The stupid trespassing mailman had put him in this predicament. "Then do what with her? Send her priority mail to the morgue?"

"You got a swamp behind your house, Bob. Use it."

Bob shook his head. He couldn't believe the mess he was in. But as crazy as it sounded, Mel was right; his fingerprints were all over the dead body. Things looked bad for him, and the cops would be at his house any second.

He grasped the goth chick beneath the armpits and dragged her face down across the basement. The dismembered ear plopped out of her mouth, but Bob paid it no mind, knowing he had little time to dispose of the body. He was glad she was a lightweight. When Mel stepped back, Bob picked her up and dropped her in the box.

Mel handed Bob the utility knife. "Here. The lid might not be a snug fit. You might have to trim the edges."

**W**hen Bob grabbed the handle, Mel seized the other man's wrist and thrust it upward. The blade punctured a hair beneath Bob's Adam's apple. Mel swiped Bob's hand across his neck, slashing his throat. Bob's body crumpled into the empty cardboard coffin.

Mel slipped on his bifocals, walked upstairs, and exited through the patio door. Nonchalantly, he rounded the small willow-lined swamp camouflaged behind the foliage and crossed the neighbors' yards. At the end of the murky shoreline, he ducked alongside Mrs. Martin's giant lilac bush and followed it all the way to his mail truck.

He climbed into the driver's seat and shifted in reverse. He slapped Herb's flag down, grabbed the bills, and left a piece of mail.

Herb, puffing on his pipe, frowned as he stepped out on his front steps and watched Mel drive away. What had come over the man? Had he finally realized his wife was tipping the scales and heeded the friendly advice?

Herb walked down the drive to the mailbox and opened it. A crumpled piece of paper lay inside. He removed it and read the note.

The same exact note he had read earlier at Bob's.

Herb grinned. "Very funny, Bob. Very funny."

He chuckled all the way to his front steps. He paused when sirens split the air and squad cars parked at the end of Bob's driveway. His pipe fell from his lips, spilling burning tobacco like blood.

# THE FIRST SNOWFALL
## Boyd Reynolds

*This story is dedicated to my mom—for letting me stay up late to watch movies and TV shows I probably wasn't supposed to as a child.*

"**W**e've found it!"

The two lovers crouched low, peeking through the wiry branches at the ramshackle house only fifty strides away. Each looked at their prize in wonder; it had been an arduous journey to get there. Days previously, they had turned twenty, marking it a solid decade since they had looked for the elusive house.

"Bridge, do you think it'll be in there?"

"Of course," Bridgette snapped at Joshua. "We've been looking for this our whole lives, the parts that mattered anyway."

It was true. Their life as a couple hadn't begun until the previous year, but Joshua had followed Bridgette from the moment they met as ten-year-old kids in grade school. That was when she told him of the house. And every year since, they'd sneak into the forest at first snowfall, wishing they could find it.

Finally, they did.

Joshua stared at her face, contorted as if she'd just eaten the sourest lemon. Something about her made him fearful, a constant tremor running through each of his cells. She was dangerous, but that drew him to her.

Quietly, she shifted her irritated gaze from Joshua to the house. The night wind howled through the trees while she watched, blowing her long golden hair and whisking strands around her face. But her gaze never broke. She wanted what was in that house. It was what dreams were made of.

The three-level house had several large windows except for a single window beneath the lone, snow-covered peak on the top floor. Golden light flickered from the top floor window. Bridgette's heart skipped with delight. The sun had been down for hours, and there was no mistaking where the light came from.

"It's still there," she said. A child-like grin widened across her face. "All the riches we can dream of are up in that room."

"Do you think she'll be there?" Joshua asked, wiping snow from his short black hair.

"Don't be absurd," Bridgette said. "She'd be long dead by now."

While her words were certain, a smidge of doubt crept across Bridgette's lips. What if dead didn't mean dead? She brushed aside the conflicting thought while she made her way past the remaining branches. "Let's get what we came for."

Rumors of the house had surfaced in northern Maine during the late 1800s. The mutterings became legend, a fairytale for dreamers who, for the next one hundred plus years, would give anything to win its lottery. And fate finally brought Bridgette and Joshua to its front door.

Joshua followed Bridgette as he always did. Whatever she said, he would do, no matter how foolish or dangerous. It was something he seemingly had no control over, and she knew it. It was what drew her to him. She liked being the one in control.

A light snow began. The abandoned house looked welcoming despite gray clouds that echoed the darkness of the brick home. The dusting of snow was like a pleasant sugar coating over the stark roof, barren ground, and dense trees. The snow made everything so bright that their eyes watered. When they walked across the snow, it crunched beneath their feet, and their warm winter coats crinkled with each step.

Their footprints in the unmarred snow made a direct path to the front of the house. Determined, Bridgette led the way. Joshua trolled behind and was glancing at the sky when he saw her.

Standing in front of the lone window of the highest room was a woman. She was old. Ancient. As old as time. Her skin was ashen, her mouth as tight as a hardened red scar. A bolt of fear and excitement sparked in Joshua's heart.

He breathed it in, welcomed it, and to his surprise, he liked it. A golden light was behind the old woman, but before he could alert Bridgette, the light was snuffed out and the figure disappeared. That pleasant sensation still coursed through his body, but he wouldn't share this new feeling with Bridgette. She would crush it. The image haunted him with each step while he followed her.

Bridgette turned to look at him with her usual disdain. "See anything interesting?"

"No . . . nothing," he muttered. "Why?"

"No reason. You have a stupid smile on your face."

"Just enjoying the weather, I guess." He hoped she wouldn't pursue her question. Happily, she didn't. All she wanted was her prize, and for the first time, so did Joshua.

The great home loomed over them, towering like a bricks-and-mortar giant. The long windows gazed down, lit up with the reflection of the snow like the whites of eyes.

The couple proceeded to the front of the house and ascended the snowy stairs to the weathered porch. When they reached it, the porch lay empty; a large red door greeted them.

Bridgette stopped directly in front and removed her glove. An icy chill ravaged her skin. Reaching forward, she put her palm on the door and smiled at Joshua. "It's warm."

He grinned. Many years previously, the two had stumbled upon an old etching in Bridgette's grandfather's attic, which told of a house that held the greatest wealth in the world. In that house a golden, unnamed treasure resided in the top room, but only to the first person to claim the seat and wait for the heart's desire to be revealed. The treasure was fickle, only appearing to those seeking it during the first snowfall. And only if the front door was warm.

Bridgette pushed the door. It opened. When she entered, an odor so strong engulfed her that she fell to one knee. Joshua sprang to her side, clasping her hand.

She looked at him with fire in her eyes and snatched her hand back. "Don't ever do that again!"

"I thought something happened to you."

"Don't worry about me. Worry about yourself." She looked around, taking another deep breath. "This place? There's something wrong with this place. Can't you feel it?"

Joshua stopped. "I don't feel anything." He was lying; he did feel it, but it was not the horrid feeling that Bridgette obviously felt. This was something he had never experienced. For the first time, he felt true love.

Both quiet, Joshua and Bridgette continued into the front room, which was filled with elaborate furniture from another time. Couches, chairs, shelves, and décor. Everything appeared to have been dropped there from the grandest antique store—from tufted-velvet, throne-like armchairs to ornate, tarnished-silver candleholders. Although the room was dark, it looked as if a maid had just cleaned it. It was an immaculate museum.

"This can't be right," Bridgette said, breaking the silence. "This shouldn't be like this. If this house has been here for this long—"

"And what's a house that's been around for a hundred years, yet only appearing on the first snowfall, supposed to look like?" Joshua countered.

Bridgette gaped in wonder and rage at him. She had never been interrupted by him before. Something in him had changed.

"Let's get a move on and make our way to the top." Joshua pointed at the lengthy spiraling staircase in the middle of the room.

Bridgette was still in shock when he passed her. She almost lashed back at him for speaking to her like that, cutting him so deeply that he'd cry for a week. But oddly, they needed to keep moving. Even when upset, Bridgette was cunning and that trumped everything else. "Let's get a move on then."

She pondered how Joshua had changed. He wasn't his quiet, meek self anymore—not in the house at least. He was stepping forth to inherit the prize. Her prize. She feared not having her pet to boss around, but there wasn't time to dissect or rebut his challenges. She had her fortune to find.

Joshua looked up at the spiraling staircase. Made of black twisted metal, it looked like a spider's web winding its way to the top, waiting to snare its victims.

As she had always done, Bridgette pushed herself past Joshua and climbed the stairs. She looked down at him from several strides ahead. "Now what are you going to do? Just stand there? What we both came for is up here." She looked away and stormed up the staircase, her boots dropping bits of snow on Joshua, who chased her.

"It's at the top," her voice echoed.

The long staircase circled up and up, cutting right through the other three levels of the house until it reached the peak. While she ascended, Bridgette felt claustrophobic—the black metal of the stairs closed in on her like an iron maiden. But with an emboldened Joshua right behind her and the treasure waiting, she pushed through the thought. She didn't have time for weakness.

Finally, they reached the top and stepped on a small ledge that led to a single door.

"This is it," she said. "It has to be."

She touched the door. It didn't feel like hard wood. It was softer, like living tissue. Removing her hand, the door swung open with ease. She reached into her pocket for the flashlight. Flicking it on, she scanned the room. At the very end of a long, narrow room was an old rocking chair that quietly moved back and forth. Bridgette was certain an old woman sat in the chair, hunched over while she rocked, but after her gaze slipped to Joshua moving close behind her, the woman was gone.

Bridgette entered the room, dimming the flashlight. Joshua followed, his heavy boots clunking on the wooden floor.

"This is what we came for?" she asked. She felt the warmth of the room.

"It's beautiful," Joshua said.

Bridgette turned to look at him. "It's only a chair. That's it. There better be something more. I've wasted ten years of my life waiting for this."

"Don't you see it, Bridge?" he said, almost in a trance. "Don't you see her?"

Fear leapt into Bridgette's heart. Her face turned pale. She had only seen that look on Joshua's face for her. He'd never looked that way for anyone else. Desperately, she faced the chair. "There's nothing here. We've wasted it."

"No," Joshua said with a quiet confidence, "you're wrong. You just can't see it. But it's here. It's all here!"

"You're crazy," Bridgette said. But she remembered the old etching in her grandfather's attic and what it stated: The one who sits in the chair and waits will be given what every human desires.

She looked back at Joshua, lost in his own delusion. Maybe he could see it though she couldn't.

Suddenly, a power surged through her, hitting her like a gale force wind, and snared the darkest parts of her heart. *He wants it,* she thought. *He wants all of it for himself. I've been a fool taking him along. He played me. His loving, doting act was just that.* Her eyes turned to steel when she looked at his foolish smile one last time. He was up to something. Whatever was on that chair, she had to have it.

She charged as hard as she could for the chair, her boots pounding against the floor. But halfway across the floor, her legs collapsed and she slammed her elbows and chin on the hardwood, dropping her flashlight, which rolled out of her reach. Turning over in pain, her chin bleeding and her elbows aching as if poked with red-hot coals, she looked up to see Joshua.

He had tackled her, wrapping his arms around her legs like a python. His face had turned rabid. He wanted whatever was on that chair as much as she did.

She lifted her torso, unleashed her claws, and swiped at his face. Her long nails dug into skin, slicing four long gashes.

He didn't flinch. The power that filled him with each breath was different than what had taken hold of Bridgette. A sly smile crept across his mouth when his tongue caught the trickle of blood dripping off his nose. He tasted it with delight, and then Bridgette knew. A monster had been unleashed when they entered the house. It had grabbed hold of them, but only one could claim the prize to stop it. The greed for what lay on that chair was too much to turn away from.

Blood poured down Joshua's face and into his eyes, and his grip on her legs loosened. She broke free and dove for the chair, but her boots were covered in Joshua's blood, and the moment she started running, she slipped. She knew he would pounce on her in seconds. A few feet from the chair, she turned to look at him. A golden light surrounded him. He leapt cat-like toward her. Her one-time lover's once-good heart had been penetrated by something more powerful than her manipulation. And it had turned him into something she didn't recognize.

He flung himself at her, using his hulking body to force her shoulders down and pin her. She squirmed, but it was no use. He had her. He grabbed her golden hair and smashed her head on the floor. Dazed, she reached for anything; her fingertips almost touched the base of the chair. He pulled her back to him. A gruesome scream consumed the room when he yanked clumps of her bloodied hair. Her cries pumped his poisoned heart more, venom coursing through his veins when he squeezed her neck.

With his grip tightening, the life drained out of her body. She tried desperately to grasp molecules of air. Her mind raced, knowing this would be her end, but the cunning inside her had one last idea. Her lips pressed tightly, trying to get the words out. She sputtered but finally gasped: "I . . . love . . . you."

She stared at him, releasing her hold on life, submitting to his will. And as she had hoped, he slowly released his hands. To be told that she loved him as he had told her countless times was what he'd always wanted to hear. His grip loosened more. She'd never forget that moment, one he'd never remember.

Reaching to her side, her fingertips touched metal. His beaming eyes gazed down on her when she tightened around the cold cylinder. In a flash, she clocked him on the head with the flashlight, shattering not only the glass in the flashlight but the bones around his temple, which flew like torpedoes into his brain. His loving face changed to a vacant stare when he fell, lifeless at her side.

The room fell silent. A horrible feeling blanketed her while she lay on the floor, gasping for breath. But she quickly kicked it off. It had to be done. He helped get her this far, but there was no time for sentimentality. There was still her prize to take.

Bridgette stood, her head and neck dripping with her blood. She stumbled, but cast herself into the embrace of the chair.

She sat and waited. Joshua's lifeless eyes stared at her. Everything sunk in while tears formed in her eyes. When she remembered the horrible things she'd done, it became worth it. Finally, she felt wonderful, as if her body filled with a great wealth, like being drowned in gold. She had never experienced anything similar.

And then circumstances became clear. She had all that was gold. The thought frightened her, and when she attempted to get out of the chair, she couldn't. Her hands, arms, and legs were cemented to the chair. Panic settled in, but it was no use. She was fused to the old rocker.

The golden light Bridgette and Joshua had seen when they first viewed the house from the trees materialized. The image emerged from within the chair and the shape of an ancient woman formed. Smiling, she stood in front of Bridgette.

"Thank you, my dear. Thank you." The woman's voice was as sweet as apple pie on a Sunday afternoon.

"What are you talking about? What is happening? I can't get off this chair."

"Of course you can't," the golden woman said. "But that is why you are here. You came for the ultimate of riches."

Bridgette sat silent.

"I am here to give it to you, just as someone a hundred years ago was here to give it to me. I bestow on you what all mankind, or womankind in your case, wants most of all—time. The most precious thing in the world is not money or jewels or even power. What everyone really wants is time, and that's what you'll have. You'll have all the time in the world sitting in this chair. You will only be released from this room when another just as greedy as you comes looking. Only then will you be like me, free to fly away." The old woman floated above the floor and through the single window in the room. As she dissolved through the glass, the gold turned to dust and collected in a small pile on the floor.

Bridgette sat, alone with a corpse, a pile of gold, and—worst of all—herself.

# SHOW COOKING – CANNIBAL EDITION
## Kev Harrison

**W**hat exactly would you have done in my position?

She'd been explicitly clear. I remember the sound of her voice when she framed the words with her delicate lips: "Take your eyes off my little display for even a second, you little shit, and you will be next."

That was not what I'd expected when I'd offered to help the lady with her shopping hours earlier. Mum and Dad always said I should respect my elders and help them if they were in need. So that's what I'd done.

But since that day, I've never fancied shepherd's pie.

***

**"C**an I help you with them bags, madam?" I asked in my politest voice when I saw her stagger, packhorse-like, down the disabled ramp at the front of Asda. I'd been riding my skateboard around the carpark, trying (and mostly failing) tricks and grinds on the low walls and trolley rails. Oh, how her eyes lit up.

"Such a polite young man," she said, which made me beam. Being called "young man" rather than "boy" at eleven is a feat.

She handed me one of the bags, the biggest one, stuffed to bursting with butter, spuds, and veggies. I won't lie—it was bloody heavy, pardon my French—but I'd offered. Was doing a good deed. Would tell Dad about it. He might even buy me an ice cream.

"Where to then, madam?" I asked as we waddled along the pavement that swept out from the Asda carpark and over the little brook toward the park.

"It's through the park, my dear. A little cottage. Maybe you've seen it when you've been out playing with your friends?"

I shook my head. "Dunno, madam, sorry."

We strolled, not a care in the world. The sun beat down. It was the second week of my six-week school summer holiday. Life was good. We entered the park and passed in front of the gravelled kids' playground, where my friends and I dared each other to do a full loop-the-loop on the swings. Daryl always said he'd done one when he was there by himself, but we all called bullshit on that.

The woman and I followed the long path into the fringes of the trees where some of the sunlight was blocked out, cooling the air a little. Birds squawked at both sides of the footpath. That angry call that blackbirds make when you're on their patch. I mimicked back to them in my best blackbird voice.

"May I ask your name, young man?" the old lady asked cheerfully, interrupting my bird conversation.

"I'm Tom, madam. Can I ask yours?"

"Rosina. Pleasure to meet you." She nodded, her hands busy with her bags.

I nodded back.

"That foreign, madam?" I asked. "If you don't mind me asking, that is." I felt my cheeks flush. Perhaps that was an impolite question.

The old lady chuckled, much to my relief. "It is. How perceptive of you! It's German. My parents were German. But they're gone now."

"Sorry, Rosina." I patted her arm in what must have seemed like a very patronising gesture.

We walked in silence.

"Here we are then," she said finally.

In front of us was a cabin or a hut. Some kind of wooden building. It certainly didn't look like anything I'd have called a home. Not in mid-1990s England. Moss-covered dark wood made up the whole structure, a single storey bungalow little more than a lean-to with a heavy door in the main façade. But she was old. Maybe she'd been there a long time. I tried not to show surprise on my face at the state of the place.

"Where shall I leave the bags, madam? Inside? In the kitchen?"

She nodded and thanked me as her bony fingers fidgeted with the keys, undoing two deadlocks before finding a smaller, brass-coloured key to undo the main catch. She pushed the door, and it gave way with a quiet sigh. I stepped through the portal and was met with the smell of sweet bread. With a pinch of sugar to make the dough irresistible. My stomach rumbled. Embarrassed, I pressed my belly.

"Not had lunch yet, Tom? Do you fancy one of my currant buns?"

When I entered the kitchen, I almost dropped the bag of shopping. Six freshly baked currant buns sat on a cooling rack on the table. Fat and ever-so-slightly browned on top, with fluffy white dough underneath and dotted with plump, juicy raisins. I licked my lips.

"Well, Mum says I shouldn't." But my resistance was weak. I opened my palms, and Rosina placed one of the lukewarm rolls on them. I ripped a piece from one side and put it into my mouth. I chewed. Flavours of cinnamon and raisin danced on my palate.

I followed old Rosina's direction to sit at a chair, which had been angled away from the kitchen table. I ate and watched as she put away the things, first from the bags she'd carried and then from the one I'd brought for her. Her kitchen, despite all suggestions to the contrary from outside, was magnificent. Homemade jams filled the cupboards to bursting, and huge balls of cheese and cuts of cured meat littered every shelf of the fridge.

But I couldn't stay long. I'd told Mum I'd be back for lunch by two. It had to be half one already. I stuffed the last chunk of bun into my mouth and chewed vigorously. "Thanks so much, Rosina, but I have to be getting back."

"Thank you, young Tom. You're a strong fellow, and I'm quite sure I'd have struggled home without you." She took her small framed glasses from the bridge of her nose and cleaned them on a cloth from the sideboard.

"Oh, madam, there's one thing. Can I use your loo? Beg your pardon."

She smiled that warm smile again. "Of course you can. Go out of the kitchen, walk down the hall, and it's the first door on your left, near the back door."

She whistled as I walked away from the kitchen. I heard the clanging of pans and shopping being stuffed away in its rightful place as I peed. Then I heard a crash. I shook the drips and did up my shorts, washing my hands before I left the cupboard-like toilet.

"Is everything all—" The question died on my lips. Rosina stood at the kitchen table, holding a butcher's cleaver. At her right, a man sat on a chair, similar to the one I'd been sitting on.

"Hello," I said and gave a feeble little wave.

The man grunted. A rag was bundled in his mouth. I stood on my tiptoes to see that his arms were tied around his waist.

"Rosina, who's this man?"

"Would you do one more thing for me while you're here, seeing as you're such a good lad, Tom?"

This probably wasn't going to be something good, judging from the situation. "What do you want me to do, madam?"

"Only to watch."

"Okay. But ... err ... What am I watching?"

"This man has been making trouble. Now I'm going to cut him into tiny pieces. Then I'm going to mince him and make him into a shepherd's pie."

"Mum says it's only shepherd's pie if you use lamb." This might not have been the appropriate thing to say. Fortunately, it caused her only to laugh. The man, far from laughing, was quite red in the face and sweat was beading up on his forehead. I dug my hands into the pockets of my shorts so she couldn't see me balling and unballing my fists.

"Is this a game, Rosina?" I lolled forward on my tiptoes again to get another look at the rope. It looked awfully tight.

"It *is* a game, Tom. That's exactly what it is. The game is this. You watch me slice and dice this gentleman and I'll let you walk free. But take your eyes off my little display for even a second, you little shit, and you will be next."

I was a bit startled. First, because what she suggested was crazy, and secondly, because she'd called me a little shit when I'd been extremely helpful. "I don't think I want to play this game, to be honest. I think I'm just going to go."

I walked to the front door, picked up my skateboard, and tried the catch. The door didn't budge. I turned my head. "Rosina, you put the deadlocks on."

Her angular, withered face crept around the kitchen doorframe until her eyes were locked, laser-like onto mine. "Yes. Yes, I did."

In the light, she looked utterly horrifying. When she stepped into the hall, creeping closer to me, I saw how enormous the blade was. The edge shone, sharp enough to go straight through an arm, I reckoned. Or a leg. Probably even a neck.

"Come. To. The. Kitchen. And. Sit. Down." The spaces between the words gave each one its own weight and significance.

I wanted to go to the toilet again. I squeezed. But what could I do? I nodded and walked toward her, looking at the floor, which I suddenly noticed was filthy with mud and cobwebs. I walked solemnly into the kitchen and seated myself in the chair I'd sat in previously.

She went back to the man, who began to rock violently, forward and backward, as much as he could in the restraints. His grunting was feverish, the pitch even higher when Rosina snatched a clump of his hair and tugged back his head. She measured the middle of his neck with the blade and raised it above her head in her skeletal hands.

"Wait!"

She stopped, glaring at me.

"Can you move these buns? I'm going to be sick if I have to watch this while I smell them, right under my nose."

She placed the knife on the countertop behind her, picked up the tray of buns, and put them in a cupboard in the panel next to the cooker. "Okay?"

I gave her a thumbs-up.

She grabbed the man's hair and the blade once again, measuring the spot. She lifted the blade above her head and must have noticed me scrunch my eyes. Holding the cleaver aloft, she hissed "Two. Eyes. Open."

Bile rose at the back of my throat, but I had to do as she said. I opened my eyes, straining my eyelids so both of them were open to an exaggerated point.

The blade came down so quickly it blurred, the old woman possessing strength I'd never imagined she'd have. His head rolled off his shoulders as if he'd been no more than a mannequin, blood spraying and soaking Rosina's arm. She didn't seem to notice and, if anything, the sight spurred her on. The blade flashed up and down again, hacking at the man's neck and chest. His clothes shredded like paper under the force of the blows and razor sharpness of the blade.

Soon, one of his arms was in four pieces. Blood drenched one side of the table and oozed to the filthy floor. Every fibre of my being wanted to stop watching, but Rosina's eyes darted to mine every few seconds, the threat of my own butchery hanging over me like Damocles' sword. I watched as she finished her work with the colossal knife, dividing the man into seventeen relatively even pieces.

The head, in three parts, was barely recognizable after she scooped out the brains with an ornate-handled serving spoon from one of the drawers behind her. She gathered the intestines, reeking and steaming like out-of-date sausages, and dropped them into the bucket holding the man's stomach and chest cavity, which were cut into six pieces.

Then she set about the peeling process. My mind cast back to the time when Grandad had the bright idea of buying a live turkey at Christmas. After its beheading, my parents placed it in a steel tub in the freezing garden and patiently plucked the feathers.

Fragments of the man's clothing came off in layers, revealing bits of skin or bare flesh where the skin had been pulled off in random directions as cubes were divided from the whole.

Once she finished chopping, she dropped each meaty chunk into the ceramic basin under the window. She ran cold water, using her bare hands to rub away filth and muck from the pieces that had fallen to the ground, only superficially cleaning the others. Finally, she dried her hands and took an enormous chopping board and mincing machine, similar to ones in Fowler's Butcher Shop, from a high shelf. She positioned the mincer at one end of the chopping board and fed the first block of man into the trough at the top. Then she began to grind. Occasionally, pieces of bone were too thick and dense to go through the mincer's jaws and she'd dig her hand into the meat to rip it out. It was tiring work. The woman's hands locked up, and she flexed her fingers to get life back. I wasn't going to offer to help, though. She looked up at me a couple of times, offering me that same smile, which I was unable to return as I had previously.

With the mincing done, she stood over the cooker, heating a huge pan into which she tossed chopped onions, celery, carrots, and garlic cloves that she stirred around and around. Normally, it would have smelled wonderful, but the last thing in the world I felt was hunger.

She fed in the meat, bit by worm-like bit, until the entire man was in the great pot. She stirred it, sniffed it, tasted it. She added this and that. Seasoning here, tomato paste there. Finally, she tipped the huge pan and levelled it into the base of an enormous roasting dish. She slathered on a thick layer of mashed potatoes from a casserole dish behind her, which I'd failed to notice, smoothing it over with a spatula.

"What do you think?" she said, as she turned up the oven to 180 degrees.

I sat in silence. What was I supposed to say? Blood still oozed down the wall on the other side of the kitchen.

"Looks ... erm ... looks good. Can I go, please?"

"Yes, dear. You did very well. Kept your side of the bargain. Don't tell anyone about any of this, or I *will* find you. You understand me?"

A grit appeared in her voice that had been absent hours previously in front of Asda. I shook my head, vigorously. I wouldn't say a word; I just wanted out. "I do have one question, if you don't mind?"

She nodded.

"Who was the man?"

"Estate agent," Rosina said, unflinching.

"Dad says they're all bastards."

"All bastards." She nodded in confirmation. She lifted her apron over her head and walked with me to the door. She unlocked the two deadlocks and swung the door back, motioning for me to leave.

I moved to shake her hand but remembered the sight of blood soaked up to her elbows and beyond. I withdrew my hand. "Thanks for the bun, madam. See you."

She closed and locked the door behind me.

# EYES WIDE OPEN
## S.T. Himmonds

**W**hen the doorbell shrilled, Lisa's eyes widened and she flinched, but she quickly motioned for her son, Jamie, to stay on the couch. She tiptoed to the front door and peeked through the peephole, leaping back at the sight of magnified eyes, fearful for an instant the individual had seen her, but she knew he—or she—couldn't. After the peephole had been installed, Jamie stood on a chair inside the house looking through the glass while she peered in from outside.

But had the person at the door heard movement? Or seen lights?

She doubted anyone could detect the low volume on the television, and the inside houselights were off and the drapes pulled snug. The small glow from the nightlight and the television, both of which faced the opposite wall, were so faint as to be negligible.

After ringing the bell another time, the individual banged on the door, and Lisa shifted farther back, worried the door might break from its rusty hinges.

Jamie sprang to his feet and stood like a tin soldier at attention. Tousled chestnut hair covered his forehead. His eyes bulged. Despite the dim light, Lisa saw the sheen of sweat on his tannish skin and the light puckering of his thick lips.

Her heart beat erratically. *Thump. Thump. Thump.*

She stepped toward her son, still cemented to the floor and swaying slightly. She pulled him against her, her hand pushing his face into her side. Despite being short and slight for his age, he was healthy and strong.

"Let's go upstairs," she whispered.

He nodded, and they crept up the stairs. The doorbell rang several more times, along with persistent pounding. At that rate, Lisa thought, the door would definitely collapse and the intruder would gain access.

She led Jamie into her bedroom and to the walk-in closet. Recognition dawned on his face, and he slumped. "No, not just me, Mommy."

"Yes, you."

She pulled the five-foot-high chest of drawers away from the wall, an effortless and soundless motion since it sat on a throw rug, to reveal a two-foot square door. She slid her finger into the small hole in the thin wood door and swung it open. "Come on, Jamie, don't give me a hard time."

He cowered between her dresses and skirts at the opposite side of the closet. "Can't I hide here instead?"

"No, this is safer."

"It scares me in there. It's so dark."

They'd had a trial run. Several of them.

"I have a flashlight, remember?"

He nodded but wasn't convinced.

"Come on," she hissed, motioning to the opening in the wall, "we're wasting time."

Jamie peeked from between the clothing and stumbled toward his mother. She bent to grasp him against her. He trembled, and she rubbed his back. "Just for a little while, sweetie. I promise."

She released him, and he crawled into the cubbyhole. She withdrew the flashlight from the top drawer and flicked it on. "See, still works."

He positioned his knees against his chest, wrapping his arms around them, and reached for the flashlight with his right hand.

Lisa attempted a smile. "I promise I won't be long. But you promise me, too. Don't leave the room until I come back and give the okay. You promise?"

He trembled and tears welled, but he nodded again.

"Say it: 'I promise I won't leave the room.' And no fingers crossed either."

"I promise," he mumbled. A tear slid down his cheek. "I don't like it in here." He glanced around. "It's scary. And small. And it'll be dark when you shut the door."

Jamie wasn't claustrophobic, but he frightened easily. What little kid didn't, she reasoned, especially in the position she placed him. But he trusted her. And she was certain he'd be safe.

"I'll see you soon. I promise." She blew him a kiss and held back her own tears.

She pushed the door shut and shoved the chest of drawers back against the wall, making it almost impossible for Jamie to open the door. She'd painted the chest, which was wide enough to cover the opening, the same beige as the shelving in the closet. No one could possibly know the piece of furniture had been an afterthought.

She adjusted necklaces hanging from hooks on the figurine that sat on the bureau top and centred the doily beneath the ornament. Perfect. Nothing out of place.

Though she'd been upstairs for mere minutes, she felt as if she'd been there for hours. But no matter how long she'd been gone, the intruder had ample time to enter the house if that's what he'd wanted. She breathed deeply, glanced at the hidden niche, and closed the closet door behind her.

Lisa had purchased the property the previous year, after she and Ben separated. The house was small, with only two bedrooms, but the rooms were large. Spacious plots of land—as well as vengeful people—had driven her to the country, where Jamie had room to roam and where they'd be safer. Ben had remained in town.

At the time, she thought the house was far enough away from town that people would forget she had ever existed. She was happy to be out of Avonport, where townsfolk remained stuck in another era as if time had passed them by. Shoeless wives obeyed their husbands. Frilly white aprons covered women's flowery dresses, and flowing dresses masked bulging bellies.

At first, she'd been scared living out of town without another adult and regretted the purchase. Renting would have been a better option, but at the time, she figured she was stuck in the area no matter the issues. Ben wouldn't relocate, and she didn't want to move away from him or Jamie, nor could she separate father and son. She lived mainly off assistance from Ben, and she and Ben shared custody of Jamie. Jamie adored his father and vice versa.

After she moved in, she had been elated to discover the little hideaway off the closet. She'd told no one about it—not even Ben. It was hers and Jamie's secret. Jamie loved secrets, and at the discovery, his face glowed sharing what only one other person knew. The cubbyhole resulted from the construction of the dormer window, but it would be impossible for anyone in the bedroom to discern such a dead space was accessible through the closet. Lisa had thought it an ingenious idea to place the chest against the wall to mask the opening.

She crept downstairs. A chill swept over her, bumps appearing on her skin like hives. Itchy, like creepy crawlers under her flesh.

And creepy creatures at the door.

The intruder knew she was home. Of course he did. And most definitely the person would be male.

Though the ringing of the doorbell and the pounding on the door had begun months previously, the occurrences had increased within the last two weeks, but whenever she answered the door, a deserted porch faced her. Jamie was becoming as scared as she was. And that was when she'd devised the makeshift panic room and convinced him that's where he'd go whenever the incidents happened. Other than trial runs, this was the first time he'd actually been holed there—the first time she'd been this frightened.

The doorbell peeled again when she reached the bottom tread. Her heart pounded as loudly as the doorbell, thrashing against her chest like a madwoman trying to escape an asylum.

She peered out the peephole, but in the dark, the face was obscured as she knew it would be. Her palms sweated. She longed to race upstairs and join Jamie in the hideaway.

"Lisa, let me in."

*Ben?* It was Ben's fault she'd been scared shitless?

She hesitated. How could she not let him in? He'd be suspicious if she didn't, but she couldn't; not with Jamie hidden in the closet. She switched on the porch light. She unfastened the chains, slid the deadbolt, and opened the door. "Ben, what are you doing here?"

Framed by darkness behind him and the overhead bulb highlighting his face, his fair skin glowed even whiter. He peeked into the house, his eyes darting about. "Jamie here?"

"Of course he's here. Where else would he be?" She rubbed her eyes. "He's in bed asleep. And so was I until you started pestering me. Christ! What's with you? You scared the wits out of me." She glared at him. How dare he frighten her like that? "Two rings are enough. If I don't answer by two, then you'll know I'm not home. Or occupied. Or something."

Ben frowned. "What do you mean? I just got here. I only rang it once."

"No, you didn't. You've—" *been pounding and pushing for ages*, she finished silently. She rubbed at goosebumps sprouting on her arms. He *had* been at the door, hadn't he?

"Is everything okay? I just wanted to see Jamie for a sec."

"I told you. He's in bed. Asleep."

Ben glanced at his watch. "It's not even eight o'clock."

Lisa sighed and breathed deeply, regretting her snippiness. If he had any inkling she and Jamie were unsafe, he'd insist they leave. He might take Jamie and not let her have him back. No, he wouldn't do that. Despite their separation, they remained close. Still in love.

"I'm sorry. I'm cranky for some reason. He wasn't feeling well. Neither was I. So we went to bed early."

"Is he sick?"

"He's fine. He was just tired. I really don't want to disturb him. It took forever for him to get to sleep."

Ben scanned her face. Could he see her fear? Could he smell it?

"Truly, he's fine. Come back tomorrow if you can." She moved to close the door, but he wedged his foot in the space.

"I just wanted to leave this." He held out a bag. "Some Lego pieces he left the other day. He can't finish the corral with missing pieces." The corral with the horses and cows was Jamie's favourite set of blocks.

"Oh, okay." Should she invite him in? No, he had no right banging on her door like that, scaring her half to death. Or had it not been him previously? She scrutinized the darkness. Was anyone else there? Nameless faces and eyes spying on her? On Ben. Had he been followed? Had the other person—or persons— at the door given up and left? Had Ben scared him—or them— away? Yes, that must be it. She was safe. They'd seen Ben and fled.

She relaxed and took the bag from him. Her fingers brushed his sleeveless arm, brown against white. "Thanks."

Ben grasped her free hand. White against brown. "You sure you're okay?" He tried to peer into the room again, but she blocked his view. Not that there was anything for him to see or not see. What the heck was wrong with him?

"I'm good. Tired. Thanks for stopping by. But please, don't keep at the door like that again. Perhaps there's a reason for not answering."

Ben frowned. His hand went to his hair. "I just—okay, whatever." He turned and then looked back. "Sure you're okay?"

Lisa nodded. She really was tired. Plus she had to extricate Jamie, hidden unnecessarily and scared out of his wits. She exaggerated a yawn. "Bye, Ben. See you later, okay?"

He nodded and waved.

She slammed the door, a little harder than she'd intended. Sighing, she switched off the light. She slid the deadbolt, reattached the chains, and pushed in the button on the doorknob. She leaned against the door. She wanted Ben so much. She should call him back. The airless, dimly lit room suddenly chilled her.

But then she remembered Jamie. He'd been in the hellhole much too long.

She headed to the staircase and had just stepped on the second tread, her other foot hanging in mid-air, when the doorbell shrilled again.

"Cripes, Ben," she mumbled, but a second later, she realized he'd answered her wish. Still, she wavered. Should she release

Jamie first and then answer the door? Ben would wait, especially after just talking to her. Or she could let him in, tell him to sit, pretend she was going to wake Jamie but instead release him. Then swear Jamie to secrecy.

But she hated lies and didn't want her son—their son—to grow up with falsehoods and secrets. No, she'd simply tell Ben to leave again. She'd be more forceful.

She shuddered at her predicament. Even though she and Ben still loved each other, they shouldn't be together. They shouldn't have had a child. She'd have to leave the area eventually. The episodes over the past few weeks had made that more than clear. She could sell the house, recoup her money, buy another. In another place, where blacks were accepted. She'd leave Jamie behind. He was much lighter than black but a couple of shades darker than white, a mix of her and Ben; people might forget he was biracial. Maybe Ben would change his mind and consider moving so the three of them could live happily ever after.

The dratted doorbell peeled again. She'd be calmer with Ben at her side. The night scared her. Even the usual state of the living room, with the television's volume turned low and the lights dimmed, added to her discomfort.

She flipped on the porch light, whipped off the chain, thrust the lock across, and the door flew open.

"What the hell—"

Torches flared inches away. One of the masked individuals grabbed her arm. Another produced a grain bag.

*No!*

The bag was pulled over her head, the fabric scratchy and musty. Dust filtered into her eyes, blinding her. She couldn't breathe. *No . . .*

Hands yanked her from the porch and down the path. *Ben, where are you? Ben, is this you? No, Ben wouldn't do this.* Ben loved her.

Jamie. *Jamie!*

Ben. Ben would save her. And he'd save his son. Ben had barely left her home. Ironic that she'd left their home seven months previously, solely for Ben's and Jamie's safety. She hadn't wanted to go too far away. Ben and Jamie were all she had in the world. Jamie needed his father as much as his mother, but the boy wasn't safe with Ben. Ben wasn't safe with his son. None of them were safe.

Ben wouldn't want her dead. It was the townsfolk. But Ben was complicit, too. He grew up in Avonport, Alberta, where everyone knew everyone, and he married her. She birthed a bi-racial child. *But this is 1978*, she screamed. *Things should be better. We're not in the fifties and sixties any longer. People should be able to marry whom they choose. Whites should be able to marry blacks. Blacks should be able to marry whites. No,* she screamed again, wondering whether she'd merely thought the words.

They dragged her for what seemed like forever, but she knew it had been mere minutes. Too many long minutes for too many thoughts to filter through her mind. Her life. Ben's life. Jamie's life.

But Jamie was safe. Jamie would listen. He'd stay in the closet until her soothing voice told him it was okay. Until she moved away the dresser. Until she opened the cubbyhole door.

She relaxed. Ben? Ben could take care of himself. She hoped. But could he?

Had he enough time to leave her property and return to town? She didn't know if he'd walked or taken the car. It was only a fifteen-minute drive. Thirty-nine minutes of brisk walking. Shorter if half-running and half-walking. She'd done it often, mainly on the weekends when Jamie was with Ben, when she was lonely and needed human contact. In the dark, she'd slither from her house, trek through the woods, scamper across the open field, and race into town while hiding beneath overhanging elms and behind fences. Making her way to Ben's. Had she been seen on those occasions? No, she was certain she hadn't been detected.

So why now? Except for sneaking into town to visit Ben, she'd stayed away. When she needed groceries or had medical appointments or sought a break from walls that guarded her from the outdoors, she drove to Bakersfield, over an hour away. Bakersfield's inhabitants lived in the present as they'd done for years, past horrors long ago put aside. Although they didn't know her circumstances, she'd been welcomed there as was every other person, no matter race or religion or education. Blacks lived amongst whites; whites lived amongst blacks. She'd debated moving to Bakersfield at the start, but homes were more expensive there than closer to Avonport, and she hated throwing money away on rent. For the first time, she regretted having ruled her life by money. Of course, she hadn't wanted to be that far from Ben and Jamie, either.

Half-dragged, half-walking, her bare feet scraped over brambles and stones that cut into her ankles and dug into her soles.

Abruptly they stopped. The bag was yanked from her head. She couldn't open her eyes at first. Grit clung to her lids. She wanted to rub her eyes, to clear them from the pressure, but her arms were held behind her.

She finally opened her eyes to find herself surrounded by white-robed, shadowy individuals. Flashlights flared. Torches blazed. These men—definitely men—were monsters. They were strong. They were nasty. Mean. Renegades fashioned after the KKK, obsolete for the most part since the late 1920s when they'd been known as the Ku Klux Klan of Kanada. Her father had told her stories. "You have to know the history," he'd said. And he'd relayed the story of his father—her grandfather—and how the five-year-old had watched his father flare like a flaming torch.

She glimpsed her house, a glow in the distance, the porchlight a beacon to her son, not as bright as a star, but a welcoming sight. As long as she could see her home, she'd feel close to Jamie.

Hands wrenched her backward. Something heavy and rough dropped on her shoulders.

Several figures, brandishing burning torches held high like trophies, surged away from her and headed toward her house. In their white flowing gowns, they resembled angels with too-bright halos skipping toward salvation. She watched, terrified, while the moving flames grew smaller and smaller.

Then there was nothing. The remaining individuals around her were silent. She was silent. Wondering. Watching.

And then the men hooted and howled. And distant flames surged. Tiny flashes of light around her house that started small and grew larger, higher and higher, crawling up the ancient timbers.

Her eyes widened. *Jamie!* Had she spoken? No, she couldn't. Her mouth was too dry. And she couldn't give her son away.

Ben! *Ben, save your son.*

Ben was safe. He'd protect them both.

Jamie. He'd obey her. He'd stay in the closet until she said it was safe. No! For once he shouldn't listen to her. Why couldn't he be a bad boy? Why couldn't he be older, stronger? He'd sense danger if older. He'd push open the door, thrust aside the chest of drawers, and emerge into the closet. He'd smell flames, go to the back window, drop three feet onto the storage roof. He'd jump from there to the ground and run. And run and run. He'd be smart enough to race to Bakersfield, where he'd be safe, instead of to his father's. Someone would take him in. Feed him, clothe him. And when the truth came out, he'd be back with his father. He'd be fine.

But—no, she'd told her son to stay put. He wouldn't budge; he wouldn't be able to.

Her head yanked backward, the noose tightening around her neck. She couldn't breathe.

They pulled her farther into the woods.

The trees! She faced certain death by a thick, stately oak with sturdy branches. But it only took one. Just one fat, protruding limb.

They tossed the rope over the branch. Once, twice. Third time a charm. They tied one end of the rope to the tree. A man, shrouded with the Klan robe, Canada's maple leaf embroidered opposite the cross insignia, pulled the other end to tighten the slack from the tree. To her neck.

They yanked the rope until she stood taller, both feet on the ground. The noose tightened. She stretched on tippy toes.

And then she saw him. A mirage? A miracle?

Two white-clothed men escorted Ben toward her.

All would be fine. Ben would save her. And Jamie. *Ben, get Jamie.* She vocalized her words. *He's in the closet, in my bedroom.*

But no, she could barely breathe. She couldn't speak. She tried. Oh, how she tried.

And then they grasped Ben. And produced another rope.

*No, not Ben, too!*

Her eyes bulged. She glimpsed her house in the distance, the flames closer to her than previously. Larger, higher and higher they went. Heat seared her body. Sweat dripped down her forehead, hitting her cheeks. Burning wood and scorching flesh invaded her nostrils.

She pictured Jamie crouched in the closet as she'd last seen him and hoped he'd fallen asleep, that his head rested on the pillow and the quilt covered him so he wouldn't feel the fire.

---

*Although the KKK operated throughout Canada as the Ku Klux Klan of Kanada, it was most successful in Saskatchewan, where by the late 1920s its membership was over 25,000. The Klan robes in Canada had a maple leaf opposite the cross insignia. The Canadian Klans, including the Saskatchewan Klan, declined in the following decades as they did in the rest of Canada. However, in the 1970s, the Klan attempted to organize again in Canada, notably in Ontario, Alberta, and British Columbia.*

# OPENING YOUR EYES IS THE MOST PAINFUL THING YOU WILL EVER HAVE TO DO

## Tom Johnstone

There was no one else in the bus shelter when Shane Turner approached. He could get out of the rain, without bothering anyone, without anyone bothering him.

Something blocked his view of the timetable. A sticker. What was left of the sticker. Someone had gone to a lot of trouble to remove it, but their best efforts had failed to erase it entirely. White strips clung to the transparent plastic that protected the timetable, where a key had scraped away the glued-on paper. Random words and fragments of words remained: peni . . . the . . . painf . . . you . . . do . . . eat . . . Ch . . . Cr . . . , along with a disturbing yet compelling picture.

The image showed a pale, naked figure, its face a white, featureless blur. Someone had slashed a razorblade across the area where one of the eyes had been. Black blood flowed from the wound.

Shane looked away from the sticker, yet he found his eyes drawn back to it. There was nothing much else to see. The rain persisted, drenching the street in a fine mist that obscured almost everything. When would the bus arrive? Soon, he hoped. He didn't want to look at the image again, to try to peer past it to view the timetable. The picture turned his stomach yet reached out to him, touched him with a queasy fascination.

He shuffled away from it to the other end of the shelter, where another almost identical sticker waited. It would have been identical, but the key had scraped away different parts of it, so different words were missing: Open . . . eye . . . you will ever d . . . Chur . . . of Creat. . . . Different parts of the image were visible, too. He saw the heroically muscular arm wielding the open razor but not the wound.

He returned to the previous sticker that covered the timetable and rubbed at the tatters as if finishing its removal would make the meaning clearer. It would certainly make the timetable clearer.

He felt the warm breath on the back of his neck before he heard the soft voice.

"What are you doing?"

Shane spun around. A short man with pale-blue eyes and thinning, crumpled grey hair stood before him. His brown tweed jacket smelled of rain and pipe tobacco. The man's bottle-green tie made Shane think of golf clubs. He compared the stranger's outdated polished brown shoes to his own sodden trainers that had once been white. The man's ensemble made Shane's grey jogging bottoms and black hoody scruffier than usual. Rivulets of rainwater tracked down wrinkles in the man's pink face. The colour seemed to have seeped into the whites of his eyes, making their edges pink, too.

"Nothing," Shane mumbled. Why was he acting guilty? He'd done nothing wrong.

The man's eyes narrowed, but his mouth turned up at the corners, the ghost of a smile. "No," he said at last. "You don't look like one of those who try to suppress creativity and free expression. Shall I tell you what it would say if it were complete?"

Shane wished someone else would arrive at the bus stop or that the bus would appear. Nevertheless, he was curious.

"It should say: 'Opening your eyes is the most painful thing you will ever have to do.'"

"Oh," Shane said, peering into the misty rain to see if he could see anyone.

"Some people don't want to open their eyes," the man continued, "so we try to open them for them. They don't like us doing that—"

Thinking of the open razor, Shane could see why.

"—so they try to shut us up, to suppress the truth, to stifle our creativity. That's how the Nazis got started. Do you want to join us?"

"Oh, er . . ."

Shane wouldn't have called himself a joiner though he'd done all right at craft and design in school.

"It's time to take back our country. Are you with us or against us?"

"Well . . ." Shane was curious despite his misgivings. It was partly this curiosity, partly the man's soft and insistent voice, partly his desire to get rid of the man, which made him accept the offer of a small scrap of paper with the time and venue of the meeting written in neat, cramped handwriting.

*** 

The thought of the man in the tweed jacket returning was only one of the reasons why Shane was glad to see the girl (Stacy, he thought her name was) the next time he waited at the bus stop. With someone else there, the man could not corner Shane the way he had previously, standing too close, speaking in his soft, plummy voice.

Her presence made him nervous, though, but in a different way than the man had. There was no danger of her talking to him. She hardly noticed he was there, too busy with her small child, adjusting the straps on the pushchair, replacing the dummy when it fell out. He'd seen her around a few times but had never plucked up courage to speak, imagining the look of startled disdain in the hard, dark eyes on her pale face, the skin stretched taut by a severe, black pony tail—a "Croydon facelift." Strange to think she had a kid though she looked about the same age as Shane.

This situation was different. It would be silly not to say something. Yet their closeness in the confined space of the bus shelter, with the rain pelting on it, made it worse. It was similar to when his mates left him alone in a room with a girl. They were obviously trying to play matchmakers, but the silence congealed in the space between them.

It should be easy to find something to talk about, like the weather or the infrequency of the buses, but it was easier to talk himself out of it. He heard the rhythmic noise of the child sucking the dummy, saw the contrast of the faded pale blue plastic and rubber with the coffee-coloured skin of the boy's face.

Shane often daydreamed about the girl, about an imaginary "them"—him and her—but it always ended with *who was he trying to kid, thinking she'd be interested in him?* Even supposing he managed to turn that pout of dumb insolence into a grudging half smile, even if he managed to raise a twinkle in those dark eyes that reflected wired desperation, was he prepared to take on another man's boy, when he was little more than a boy himself, when anyone could see at a glance the kid certainly wasn't Shane's?

"Nice girl," a male voice murmured.

Shane turned to see the tweedy gent smiling benignly at her. Then Shane noticed his eyes dropping to the child, the corners of his mouth dropping, too, in an expression of profound distaste.

"Shame," the man muttered. "It seems *someone* got there before you."

Shane glanced round in panic, but the girl was oblivious to the man's comments, absorbed in a cigarette. The man's insinuation left a sick feeling in the pit of his stomach. She blew smoke from the dark red O of her mouth, providing a sighing back-beat to the toddler's rhythmic sucking of the dummy. Her eyes looked a little softer. Perhaps this would be the time for him to introduce himself. Relaxed by the nicotine, she might look more kindly on him.

But not with this weirdo looking on.

"Look, fella—" Shane said.

"So are you coming to the meeting, then, Mister Turner?"

Shane glanced at the girl in embarrassment. The last thing he wanted was for her to think he was the type of loser who went to meetings. She probably thought he was a loser anyway if she was even aware of him at all, which she wasn't. She was still lost in a wreath of smoke, her eyes closed, her lips parted, her expression dreamy.

He looked back at the man and remembered the scrap of paper he'd taken from him. "Yeah. Suppose so." *Anything to get rid of the weirdo.*

"Good," the man replied. "Look forward to seeing you."

After the man disappeared, as quickly as he'd appeared, into the rain, Shane wondered when he'd told the man his surname.

*** 

**W**hy had Shane agreed to go? Not that it mattered. It wasn't as if this was one of those job interviews the dole always sent him to, the ones where the employer didn't want him any more than he wanted the job but would lose his benefits if he didn't go.

On the other hand, the bloke could turn up at his home to ask why he hadn't gone. The man seemed obsessive and desperate that way, and if he knew Shane's surname, who was to say he didn't know other things about him, like his address?

Still, Shane didn't have to go. That weird old bloke with his soft, cultured voice. It wasn't as if Shane had a history of doing what people like that told him. He'd always told his teachers where to go, knowing there wasn't a lot they could do about it.

If he went, it would be because he wanted to, not because he was scared of an old creep. There'd be other people there anyway. It might be a laugh. He'd texted his mates, and no one had gotten back to him, boring bastards, so nothing doing there.

He spread out the piece of paper the man had given him and looked at the time and address written on it in the over-neat, crabbed handwriting. Its surface was rough, probably because

Shane had crumpled it into his pocket, but there was a sort of pattern to it.

He glanced around in distaste at the grey walls of his bedroom, walls that, like his trainers, had once been white. Damp bled black from the corners. That sudden sinking feeling in the pit of his stomach. He crumpled the paper into his pocket and grabbed his keys.

***

The pub was quiet for a Friday evening. A few elderly men reading the paper, a couple of younger ones playing pool around back. He looked around for the tweedy gent. Nowhere to be seen. No sign of anyone else who looked the type to attend a meeting of this sort.

Of what sort? He didn't know what the meeting was about or the people it might attract. He took the paper out again and checked the details. Yes, this was it: the Miller's Arms.

"What have you lost, love?" The barmaid looked at him with wary appraisal, hands poised over the glasses she had been on the point of stacking into a glass washer. She was probably wondering if he was underage. He wasn't, but only by a narrow margin, and he didn't have any ID with him.

"I'm here for the meeting," he said in the deepest, most adult-sounding voice he could muster.

"The South East Football Supporters' Association?"

"The what? I don't know about that."

The barmaid cocked an eyebrow as if she'd suspected the group's declared name was bogus all along.

The man had said something about "creativity" and "taking back our country." He hadn't said anything about football. The phrase "taking back our country" had stirred something in him. He wasn't a racist. He didn't hate black people. Well, no more than he hated anyone else. Yes, that was it—he hated everyone the same. He was an equal opportunities hater.

The barmaid flicked through a large red notebook full of dates and names. "That's definitely the name of the group the room's booked for. So *is* that one you want or not?" She wore the same appraising but disinterested frown.

He smiled. "Yeah, why not." He liked football. Maybe there'd be some normal people there. Maybe he wouldn't have to talk to the tweedy old bloke with the soft, insinuating voice.

She smiled back. "It's upstairs in the function room."

There was one man in the function room. So far. It was early still.

Shane wondered if the man was on the door and would demand to see proof of age. He had something of the nightclub bouncer look about him, with his shaved pink head and navy polo shirt. His pale brown slip-on suede shoes made him seem less like one, and though he sat near the door, his chair was in the row of chairs set out for the audience.

"All right," Shane said to the big bloke, who returned his greeting. "So, er . . . What's it all about, then?"

"No idea, mate, no idea. I just came to have a look."

"Me, too."

What they both looked at, Shane suddenly noticed, was a large flag or banner made from a sheet that was attached to the wall at the opposite end of the room. A large circle was painted on the sheet in thick black paint. A bright red crown perched on a large capital W written in the same stark black as the circle was inside the circle. As with the sticker, Shane found it fascinating and unsettling.

It certainly had an effect on the man in the brown suede shoes. His grey eyes were fixed on it, gazing in rapture, the pinkness of his skin seeming to seep into the whites of his eyes, like the old weirdo's.

"It's beautiful, isn't it?" he sighed.

Was the bloke on drugs? Shane should go. He needed to be pissed or stoned to enjoy something like this, and he'd run out of money and dope for the week.

Something about the image drew the eye toward it, but Shane wouldn't go so far as to say it was *beautiful*. He simply nodded back at the man's intent, pink-lined gaze.

"So why did you come?" Shane asked.

"All over the world, it's going on," the man wearing the suede shoes intoned. "Politically correct idiots censoring Christmas cards while Muslims kill Christians on our streets. It's a battle of civilisations, mate. It's time we showed them whose country this is."

Shane nodded again.

Eventually, a few people drifted into the room, all greeting the man in the suede shoes, all eyeing Shane suspiciously. None were under forty. All were men, white men. All shared the pinkish colouring around the rims of their eyes. One of them started to say what sounded like "Rahow," but the man in the suede shoes, still sitting by the door, cut him off with a sharp look and then rolled his eyes in a long-suffering fashion for Shane's benefit. Shane could have counted the number of people in that room on one hand. There was a general mutter of small talk about the weather and so on.

All conversation ceased when the man in the tweed jacket walked in.

He strode up to the podium, which stood in front of the banner. "Is the door locked, Pinkerton?"

The guy in the brown suede shoes nodded, and the man in the tweed continued. "Welcome, my friends, or should I say, congregation. For though this small room in a public house be humble, yet for now it serves as my temple, the Church of Creativity. It does not matter that we are few, my friends. Wherever two or more of us are gathered together in the sight of this banner, that place is our Church."

Shane rubbed his head and stifled a groan. He'd thought this was a meeting for football fans, but it sounded more like a God botherers' convention. Yet he listened to that insistent voice, which seemed to carry in the silent room despite its softness. The words crept into his head and made themselves comfortable in a dark corner of his brain.

"Don't worry, friends. This is not a temple to Gentle Jesus, meek and mild—that Semite! We come not to bring peace, but a sword. We're fighting a holy war to restore dignity to our country, our race!"

A few mutters of "Rahawa" or something similar that Shane couldn't distinguish interrupted the speech.

"You, me, all of us gathered here, we are all soldiers. I call on all of you to go out, fight the good fight, to turn things around in this country, with small but devastating acts of defiance. That's why I've chosen each and every one of you. I could see that you had the potential to be creatives. Now go and create."

The scrape of chairs brought Shane out of his reverie. Pinkerton had claimed to be a casual punter, but after unlocking the door, he led the "congregation" out of the room. Shane shook his head as if clearing it from the effects of a narcotic. Why had he sat there listening to this bullshit? He hadn't had a toke in weeks!

Suddenly, in a cloud of tweed, tobacco, and sweet, cloying breath, the speaker appeared beside him. "Glad you could make it, Mister Turner. My name is John Rendell, by the way, in case you were wondering. As you can see, we need more soldiers, more creatives like you. Have you still got the paper I gave you?"

Shane slowly withdrew the paper from his pocket, without having to hunt and fumble for it, prompting a murmured "Good!" from Rendell. Shane realised he had been clutching the paper the entire time, his fingers rubbing its crinkled indentations. They looked like symbols of some kind, a series of straight lines, some slanting onto others, the letters of a strange alphabet.

"Now as you are a newcomer to our little congregation," the gently persuasive voice continued, "our teachings require you to enact one or two tasks for us, so that we can be sure of your commitment. After all, you know our secrets now; you've seen our sacred symbol. You will now carry out these tasks in the presence of two adepts—"

"Tasks?" Shane looked at the door, where Pinkerton grinned back, his dark pupils and pale-grey irises gleaming within the pink-stained whites of his eyes.

"Just to prove your allegiance and show your creativity. Think of it as a dare, if you will. Do you like dares, Mister Turner?"

Puzzled, Shane glanced at Rendell. Then, as the penny dropped, a grin spread over his lean, famished jaw.

Shane loved dares as a kid though they scared the shit out of him: the awful, sick feeling when he'd scrambled up Mr. Hargrave's apple tree and nearly got caught on the wrong side of the garden fence; the bellowed threats of a burly, middle-aged man running outside after he and his mates had egged the window at Halloween, no longer interested in the treats, just in tricks. Yes, they had scared him, no doubt about that, but they'd also been the few times he'd felt alive.

While Rendell and Pinkerton escorted him toward the door, Shane glimpsed his eyes in the mirrored surface of the bar and wondered if pink lined his whites. He excused himself to go for a piss before going outside. For a minute, he thought they'd refuse his request or insist they accompany him as if they were prison guards. They didn't, though, and he examined his reflection in the mirror above the sink. He saw traces of pink in the whites of his eyes, but had they been there already, the remnants of too little sleep and a cannabis habit? Should he lock himself in one of the cubicles until they went away? No, he was curious what they wanted to ask of him.

He left the pub, flanked by the two men. The barmaid briefly looked up from her glass-washing and then carried on with a little shrug. Pinkerton opened the door of an old Rover car, and Shane slid into the back seat. Pinkerton sat beside him, which reminded him of the time the police had nicked him for shoplifting. However, this time he was getting into the car of his own free will, wasn't he?

The car rumbled through darkened streets. After a while, he realised they were familiar: the streets of his own neighbourhood. Maybe Rendell had been joking about this initiation rite thing. Maybe they were giving him a lift home. But the bloke didn't seem the type to make jokes; neither did his mate. Out of the room, Shane didn't feel quite so keen on the idea, like he'd suddenly sobered up though he hadn't had a drink. But it was too late to back out.

The car stopped by the local corner shop. Steel shutters, shining from the tarnished light of the streetlamp, had been pulled down.

"What do you want me to do?" Shane asked.

"What you must," Rendell hissed over his shoulder from the driving seat. "Be creative."

Shane hesitated. Pinkerton nudged him in the ribs, and Shane climbed out of the Rover.

The streetlamp didn't help. It made him feel more exposed. On the plus side, there was a skip nearby, loaded with rubble and other building debris. He picked up a half-brick, glanced at the shopfront, protected by the steel shutter, and then at the flat where the shopkeeper, Mr. Mukherjee, and his family would be sleeping.

Shane replaced the brick and walked back to the Rover, where Rendell glared at him.

"Can't do it," Shane said. "He's never done me any harm."

"Indeed," Rendell said. "But has he ever shown you the respect due to you?"

Shane remembered the look of contempt that had flickered across Mr. Mukherjee's face once, when Shane counted out miserable small change to buy one miserable can of cheap lager. And had there been a flicker of a smirk on the shopkeeper's face when he'd refused Shane the alcohol because he was underage?

He also remembered something from a book he'd read in school about certain animals being more equal than others. Maybe he hated everyone equally, but some people more equally than others.

He returned to the skip.

He felt a rush—one he hadn't felt for ages—when the half-brick sailed toward the pane.

He ran to the car while the sound of shattering glass tinkled in his ears.

Screams. Children sobbing. Shouts of fear and anger in a foreign tongue.

The screech of the tyres when they sped away.

They hadn't gone far before they stopped again. Why had they stopped outside this block, down the other end of the street from these flats?

Shane was still breathing hard.

Rendell sighed heavily. "You passed, Mister Turner, but only just. A little disappointing. Now, if you'd shown a little more initiative, a little more *creativity*. A petrol bomb for example. It's not rocket science, Mister Turner!"

Shane thought of the children he'd heard crying through the shattered pane, thought of the pink tinge to his eyes he'd seen in the pub mirror. What was he turning into?

*The most painful thing . . .*

"You've scraped through, but I still need more proof of the seriousness of your intent. Another test; hopefully the final one."

Rendell's veiny hand, holding what looked like a curved piece of bone, reached from the driver's seat. He dropped the object into Shane's outstretched palm.

Shane opened the razor. The blade that had been tucked into the bone handle glinted in the streetlamp's cold light.

"She should be coming out any moment for a cigarette. She always does at this time of night. But I'd have thought you knew that, Mister Turner."

The girl looked tiny and fragile in the pool of light that served the entrance to the block of flats. Pinkerton nodded toward the door.

"No, not her, not—" Shane tried to remember if her name really was Stacy.

"You don't even know her name," Rendell purred. "But you know that she's a traitor to her own kind. You know she's allowed her blood to be tainted, allowed her womb to be used as the breeding ground for a mongrel brat. Now, go to it. To show your loyalty, you have to make a sacrifice."

*The most painful thing you will ever have to do.*

Shane snapped shut the razor and stepped out of the car a second time, his legs like lead. He looked at her leaning against one of the concrete posts supporting the lintel for the entrance to the block, her eyes closed in the rapture of the smoke, oblivious to him. Oblivious to everything. If he did what the old man wanted, she'd know he was there all right. She'd have to take notice of him.

Hang on, though. What did Rendell want him to do to her? He hadn't made it clear. He'd probably tell Shane to use his imagination, his "creativity."

But he didn't have those qualities. Shane hadn't been brought up to have creativity or imagination, nor did he consider himself someone who had those things, whatever they were. If Rendell wanted something done, let him tell Shane what he wanted. In any case, his sort liked giving orders.

Shane flicked open the razor and remembered the tattered sticker stuck to the bus shelter. Had the old man meant him to act out the image on it?

Her beautiful dark eyes, mostly cold and hard but soft sometimes when she looked at her child.

*Eyes is the most painful thing you will ever have to do.*

He turned back to the car and tapped on the driver's side door. The man wound down the window.

"You want me to . . . her *eyes*?" Shane asked.

For a few seconds, Rendell's eyes with their pink-stained whites looked infinitely old and tired. Then they blazed with a sudden cold fury, and for the first time, his hitherto gentle voice hardened into a snarl.

"Look, just cut her up for me, however you want," he snapped. He muttered words sounding like "Can't get the staff . . ." to Pinkerton that drew a chuckle before winding up the window.

Something caved in within Shane. He faced the smoke-wreathed young mother and walked a few steps from the car. His gut twisted from the old man's contempt. Something stirred within the wreckage of his punctured pride: disgust, hatred, rage—the festering resentment that had built up after a short lifetime of being put down and patronised. People like that had pushed him around all his life. He'd never taken any notice of those cultured, superior voices previously. Why was he doing it now? Just because she was an easy target, someone whose life was even tougher than his?

Rendell had incited him earlier by appealing to his love of dares. Shane remembered something else about those exploits.

There'd been another kid involved, an older, intimidating kid who'd half-bullied, half-egged him on. But that fat prick had made himself scarce the time Shane got caught.

Suddenly, it struck him like the belt that had punished him for the failed dare all those years previously. It didn't matter about the girl; that he knew nothing about her, that she didn't know he existed. He loved her. Or he hated her less equally than others, which amounted to the same thing as far as he was concerned.

He turned back toward the car. Through the misted, rain-spattered glass of the windscreen the men's faces were pale, featureless blurs like the ones on the stickers, staring at him without eyes—pink or otherwise. That brief impression was dispelled when they got out of the car, and Shane saw they did have eyes after all: Rendell's flashing with disbelief, anger, exasperation; Pinkerton's gleaming with the anticipation of violence.

Shane stared back at them and then down at the open razor.

These were two men whose eyes needed opening.

Whatever he'd turned into, if he couldn't turn back, maybe he could turn it around and aim it back at its source.

# NO JOB TOO SMALL
## R.A. Goli

Jake was a man of many skills but a master of none. He'd spent years swapping one crappy job for another in an effort to keep up with the rent on his equally crappy apartment. But cleaning gutters for a creepy old lady had to be one of the worst. He cursed when he yanked another clump of leaves and mud from the guttering and tossed it to the grass below.

"Shit," he muttered, the blob missing her by inches. *How long has she been standing there?* "I'm sorry, ma'am. I didn't see you. Are you all right?"

The woman scowled at him and pointed to the muddy clod. "Don't you leave these lying all over my lawn when you're done."

"No, ma'am."

The woman huffed, turned, and walked away.

Jake watched from his vantage point on top of the ladder until she was out of sight under the veranda. He listened for the sound of the front door closing and then muttered, "Crazy bitch."

He finished the gutters and collected the mess from her precious lawn, dumping it into the garden waste bin. He packed up the ladder and went around back to wash up. The water from the outdoor tap was ice cold, and much to Jake's annoyance, it had also started to rain, which would make his drive home longer. Inclement weather, if it continued, would also affect his chances of getting more outdoor work. On the bright side, he had finished this job and could get the hell out.

Once done, he headed to the house to collect his money. He knocked at the door and waited.

"Come in," the woman's gravelly voice called.

He wiped his feet and entered the house. The woman sat in the room to his right, so he walked toward her. She was eating nuts from a bowl that sat on the lamp table, popping a couple into her mouth and feeding some to a small dog that looked as ancient as she did. He saw the dog's slobber on her fingers when she dipped her hand back into the bowl for more. Jake tried to keep his face neutral, but sticking her wrinkly, dog-drool coated fingers back into her mouth made him want to gag.

He blurted, "Nuts are no good for dogs."

"That's macadamias," she snapped. "These are peanuts."

"Oh, okay. I'm sorry," Jake said, not really knowing or caring whether that was true. "Um, so I've finished the gutters."

"Hmm, I'll get your money, then." She painstakingly got out of the armchair, the dog sliding off her lap and landing with a thump on the carpet.

Jake cringed, but the dog slowly walked away, unharmed. The old woman hobbled into the kitchen. When she returned with her purse, she thrust cash into Jake's hand. She scowled and sat back in the chair.

"Thank you." Jake left and walked quickly to his car, anxious to get home.

The rain pelted and the drive would take over an hour, but that's how desperate he'd been for the job. He started the car and accelerated, immediately feeling the sluggishness of the right side. He unrolled the window and looked out, confirming he had a flat. He didn't have a spare, having sold it for rent money the previous month.

"Fuck," he said, annoyed at his stupidity. He pulled out his cell phone to call roadside assistance, but there was no signal. *That's weird.* He hadn't noticed that earlier, not having used his phone since he left his house that morning. It seemed strange there was no service because he wasn't that far out of town. He'd have to ask the woman if he could use her phone.

He reached her door and knocked. After a few minutes, he knocked again, worrying she'd dozed off or couldn't hear him.

She startled him when she finally opened it, and her frail face peered up at him.

"I'm so sorry, ma'am. I seem to have a flat, and there's no signal on my cell. Might I use your phone to call roadside assistance?"

She stepped aside and let him in. He once again wiped his boots and walked into the hall, glancing around for the phone. He spotted it at the back of the sitting room and headed toward it.

"That phone doesn't work, but there's one in my bedroom. I'll call them for you. I don't want a strange man going in there." She headed down the corridor.

Jake returned to the hallway. He heard her voice but couldn't make out what she was saying.

A few minutes later, she returned. "They said it could take up to two hours. There's nobody in the area."

Jake suppressed an expletive and forced a smile. "Thank you. I'll go wait in my car."

"Did you hear what I said? It might be two hours. You can't sit in your car for two hours. You'll wait in here."

"I don't want to put you out."

"You've already put me out, but it's done now. Come in and sit down. I'll make some tea," she said while she wandered through the sitting room and into the kitchen.

Jake sat on the flowery couch. He felt uncomfortable, but he could hardly refuse. That would seem weird. Who would prefer to wait in a car in the rain rather than inside sipping tea?

The dog wandered over and sniffed his leg. Its fur looked lank and greasy, and it smelled like—well, like wet dog. Jake ignored the scruffy creature, and it sat in its basket.

Jake's gut clenched when he heard the kettle boil. In a few minutes she would be in the room with him, and he couldn't imagine what they would talk about for two hours. He glanced at the grandfather clock in the corner of the room, but looking at it didn't make the time move any faster.

"Here you go. I put sugar in for you already." She placed the cup on the coffee table. She set her cup on the lamp table and folded herself into the armchair.

Jake tasted the tea. It was disgusting; she must have put four sugars into it. But he drank it anyway, not daring to complain.

She watched him intently while she sipped. They didn't talk, and Jake's eyes shifted to the grandfather clock several times. The ticking echoed around the otherwise quiet room, sounding like a metronome set too low, each second taking three times longer than it should. Fifteen minutes passed before he finished his tea and placed the empty cup on the table. He glanced around the room, looking for something to talk about, when he noticed a photo of a young man of around thirty, wearing an army uniform.

"Is that your son?" he asked, feeling this was a safe topic. What mother didn't love talking about her children?

"His name was Gus. He died," she said.

"I'm sorry." He wished to God he'd not spoken nor replied to the job posting on Craigslist. The money wasn't worth this torture. He took a deep breath, suddenly nauseated. He pressed his hand against his belly and stood, excusing himself to use the bathroom. When he stepped around the sofa, he staggered, a sudden onset of dizziness overcoming him. *What the fuck?*

He looked back at the old woman, who exited her seat with the grace of a dancer, not that of a frail old woman. He glanced at the teacup. All that sugar. Was the sweetness an attempt to disguise the taste of something more sinister?

"Whalllll . . ." His tongue was thick and uncooperative. He glimpsed the phone in the corner and staggered toward it, grasping the receiver before collapsing on the musty carpet. The last thing he heard was a clear dial tone.


**W**hen Jake came to, it was pitch black. His head throbbed, and his throat felt dry. When he tried to sit, he realized his wrists and ankles were bound. He shook his arms and legs, hearing the rattle of handcuffs against the bedposts. He screamed, calling for help as loudly as his dry throat could manage, wrenching his arms and legs with all the force he could muster. After a few minutes, exhausted, he collapsed against the bed, breathing heavily.

The door to the room squeaked open and the light switched on, the glare from the naked bulb causing him to squint. He was completely naked except for a large adult diaper. The old woman carried a tray, which she placed on the side table, and sat on the chair beside the bed.

"What the hell are you doing, you fuc—" Jake's words were cut short when she shoved a pacifier into his open mouth. He gagged when the rubbery end hit the back of his throat.

"Now, Gus, behave yourself. I don't like that foul language," the woman said in a singsong voice.

Jake spat out the dummy, his face twisted in horror. "I'm not Gus. I'm Jake. The guy who cleaned your gutters." Did she have dementia or was she a psychopath?

She smiled down at him while she attached a bib around his neck. He tried to bite her hand, his teeth grazing her loose skin. She slapped him across the face.

"Stop that, Gus." She frowned, inspecting the back of her hand. "That's probably going to bruise."

"You stupid old bitch. I'm not Gus!" Panic set in.

The woman stood, waggling her finger at him. "Right, I told you I don't like that sort of language. I'd normally think washing your mouth out with soap would be a fitting punishment, but if you are going to use those teeth like that, I'll have to think of something else."

Jake spat at her, a large glob of spittle hitting her cheek. "You crazy bitch!"

His pulse quickened when her demeanor changed to the mean old woman she'd been earlier that day. She wiped the side of her face with a handkerchief and then moved down his body, undoing the diaper and squeezing his manhood in a wrinkled fist.

"Aaaaagh." Jake howled. Tears streamed down his face, the pain increasing when she closed her hand, squeezing harder.

She released him and refastened his diaper. "Now, are you going to watch your language?"

Jake said nothing. He stared at the ceiling, wondering if someone would rescue him, but he had told no one where he was going. His friends, assuming he'd taken a job out of town, wouldn't realize he was missing for months. He'd often taken work on farms or fruit picking, so his absence wouldn't seem unusual.

"It's not polite to ignore your mother, Gussy."

Jake turned to her, his eyes filled with a fear and hatred he'd never felt before. "When I get out of here, I'm going to kill you," he seethed.

She surprised him by laughing. Then she looked at him, a sly grin developing. "Oh, Jake," she whispered, "you're never getting out of here."

***

The old woman slipped her hand under Jake's pillow and pulled out a shiny coin. "Look." She held it up for Jake to see. "The Tooth Fairy came." She beamed at him, bending down to plant a kiss on his forehead.

"I'll put this in your piggy bank." She walked to the tallboy and dropped the coin into a plastic pig with the name GUS painted in amateurish lettering on the side.

Jake assumed the bank belonged to the real Gus when he was a young boy. The room, his prison, was decorated with books, toys, and posters that a ten-year-old would like.

Once a week, the woman planted a tooth under his pillow and pulled out a coin the next morning. Jake thought this was about the twelfth time, which meant he had been captive for three months. He counted days in his head by cracks of light that seeped through the curtains when the sun rose and set. But he wasn't positive because he knew she laced his food with drugs.

She had ripped out his teeth the first day, after he tried to bite her. Jake had been amazed at her strength. She told him she used to be a dentist when she was younger and still had all the tools. Age had weakened her a little, for she struggled with the roots, but she bashed those teeth with a small hammer.

A few jagged pieces of enamel remained where his molars used to be. What would happen when she ran out of teeth for the Tooth Fairy?

She slipped a hand under his buttocks. "A bit wet I see."

Jake didn't fuss anymore. Strapped to the bed, he had no choice but to wet and shit when nature called.

She wiped his urine-soaked skin with baby wipes, powdered his groin, and dragged her fingertips over his privates. "A bit prickly. I'll have to shave you again."

Jake cringed in silence. She had told him on numerous occasions that babies didn't have pubic hair.

"Now, let's eat," she said, after she fastened a clean diaper. She strapped on his bib and sat beside him. She twisted off the lid from a jar of baby food. Without teeth, that was all he could eat.

"Here comes the airplane," she said, swooping the plastic spoon to mimic a plane before heading to his mouth.

He opened his mouth. How much weight had he lost? She didn't feed him nearly enough. He watched her weathered face while he swallowed the mushy, cold spoonful, and not for the first time, wondered how old she was. He hoped she'd die soon. If she died, he would die soon after.

And then he would finally be free.

# THE DYING
## Leah O'Sullivan

Between the blinds through the frosted window, Andrea Rhodes could see the university campus. The science building sat at the top of a grassy hill that sloped down, crisscrossed by sidewalks for students to walk from building to building. Skeletal trees decorated the campus, barely grasping at the last of their color-drained leaves, most of which had fallen in clumps around the bases of their trunks. Other than the wind whistling through the grass-lined pathways, the school was silent, and bare trees were the only signs of life.

The Liberal and Creative Arts Building was across campus, the shards of its broken windows glinting in the sun. The morning was bright and cold, and beams of late autumn sunlight pierced through the cracks in the blinds and illuminated the dust floating through the air of the classroom.

"Andrea," Ari whispered, loud enough for Andrea to hear, "close the blinds!"

Andrea shut them and turned, scanning the classroom. There were five of them. Five: a decent number. You had five fingers on each hand, five toes on each foot, five bodily ways to sense the world. Five was natural. Andrea wrote a crooked 5 on her arm with a black whiteboard marker and hugged her knees, gripping the marker in her fist.

She sat in the corner of the room next to the whiteboard, where someone had written a formula containing more letters than numbers. The storage closet was at the far end of the room.

Across the room, desks and chairs that used to be arranged in neat rows barricaded the door. Ariana Platt—she preferred the nickname Ari—stood diligently next to the barricade with an ear to the wall, her clothing hanging in shreds down her long body. She absent-mindedly picked at the dried blood under her fingernails.

The siblings, Jaclyn and Long Ferrier, sat on the floor in the middle of the room and spoke in low voices, holding each other's gray hands. Alex Baumgarten sat nearby, with his legs crossed and a textbook in his lap. The cover was decorated with DNA spirals and proclaimed the title to be *GENETICS* in big, glossy letters.

"I thought you were a history major," Andrea whispered, peering over his shoulder to see layers of text and diagrams she didn't understand.

"History minor," he whispered back, not looking up from the book, "English major."

"You like books, then?"

"Usually, but I have no idea what this says." He turned a page and squinted. "I don't think I can even pronounce that word."

Andrea looked over to the Ferriers, who were now wrapped around each other. Jaclyn shook with sobs in Long's arms. "They have another breakthrough?"

Alex looked up from the textbook and shrugged. "Probably."

The Ferriers looked different enough to be strangers. Jaclyn covered herself in long sweaters and skirts as though trying to hide. She rarely spoke in class, and when she did, her voice was too soft to hear. Long, the adopted sibling, was the opposite; he'd dyed his black hair bright blue and dressed to stand out. Long didn't attend the university, but at the insistence of the Ferrier parents, he'd decided to pay his sister a visit filled with strained pleasantries, which had included Long sitting in on Jaclyn's philosophy class. However, since they were all dying, the siblings seemed to be attempting to reconcile their differences.

Ari turned to the Ferriers and put a finger over her lips. "Be quiet," she hissed, baring red-stained teeth. "You'll get the rest of us killed."

"We're dying anyway," Alex muttered, smoothing over a dog-eared corner of the page with his thumb. His pointer finger ended at the knuckle, a jagged stump that probably wouldn't grow new skin.

"You learn that in your book?" Andrea asked, but Alex didn't laugh.

This time Ari shushed Andrea and Alex, glaring at them. "Honestly, how hard is it to be quiet? Do you guys *want* to get out of this or not?"

Then, without warning, Ari's long legs collapsed underneath her when she erupted into a fit of coughs. Alex's textbook fall to the floor with a thud, and he and the Ferriers dashed over to Ari, who lay on the floor in a heap. Andrea stood carefully and peered over their shoulders to see Ari twitching and foaming at the mouth. With each twitch, something jerked inside Andrea's hollow chest, and her head spun with the voices of her peers melded together. She blinked hard, shaking her head, and when she concentrated, the world refocused and Ari had stopped twitching.

"That's it," Alex said. "She's gone."

*A*ri *flipped through her philosophy textbook and scribbled notes while the bus's movements jostled her slightly in her seat.* 3 major areas of study within ethics, *she wrote, and bullet-pointed below that:* meta ethics, normative ethics, applied ethics.

*The bus stopped at the light, and Ari glanced up, seeing her stop ahead, and tugged on the cord. The bus halted and jostled her one last time, and she told the driver, "Thank you," when she got off. She hurried to the building where the animal shelter was located, her textbook and notebook rustling inside her backpack.*

*"Sometimes I feel like you split yourself up five different ways," her mother had told her the other night when they'd Skyped.*

*"I tell you I got a great job at the animal shelter and your first reaction is maternal worry?" Ari asked.*

*Her mother had sighed. It was a familiar sound. "I know you want to save the world, Ari, but is it worth it if it means having no time to yourself?"*

Yes, *Ari had thought, but not said.* Because it's the right thing to do.

The four of them moved Ari to the far corner of the room, and Alex and Long draped their tattered jackets over her. There were other corpses in that corner, Andrea remembered; they'd moved them there when they'd first taken refuge in the classroom, but the ugly disease—virus, whatever—inside of Andrea had rotted her nose and smell nerves, so she couldn't detect the bodies rotting. Made it easier to forget they were there, she supposed.

Andrea returned to her spot by the blinds and the frosted window, noticing bloody body pieces that littered the campus. Many were grouped together alongside the academic buildings, and fewer were strewn about the crisscrossing pathways. Most of them were inside the buildings, from what she could remember, especially the residential buildings although she couldn't see those from her window.

She sat with her back to the corner where Ari lay and wrote a 4 next to the 5 on her arm. Four was a nice, even number. Four chambers of the heart, four points on a cross, four phases of the moon. The world *four* was even spelled with four letters. It was a great number.

"Now what do we do?" Jaclyn asked in a small voice from the center of the room where she sat with Long. She stared at her hands in her lap. "Ari was kind of our leader. Who's going to lead us now?"

Long squinted at something in the distance. "Alex," he said, turning to look at him, "hand me that book."

Alex furrowed his eyebrows but gave Long the genetics textbook. Long flipped through it, and then looked at the index in the back, narrowing his eyes at the words.

"Long, you're taking art classes," Jaclyn said, her soft voice muffling her condescension. "How are you going to figure something out from that book?"

"You don't have to be a bio major to be able to read a goddamned textbook," Long said, flipping a page harshly.

Jaclyn bit her lip, and Andrea guessed that if they were in any other situation, she would've added something.

"I figure," Long said, more to himself than to anyone else, while he flipped, "that Ari died in the same way Professor Hunter did. Remember? He was twitching and foaming at the mouth, too."

"If he died from a disease, you wouldn't find anything about that from a genetics textbook," Jaclyn said quietly.

Long slammed the textbook, and the noise almost made Andrea jump. "Fine, pre-med genius. Please explain how we can save our asses before the *disease* kills us, if the Feds outside don't get to us first and land bullets in our heads."

Andrea rubbed the 4 on her arm with her thumb. "I guess at this point we could just pick the more preferable way to go."

Long glared at her. "Really? You're going to make jokes? Ari's rotting over there in the corner and you're making jokes?"

"Jaclyn's right," Andrea said, unable to stop herself. "You're kidding yourself if you think a genetics textbook is going to stop us from dying. Isn't that right, Alex?" She turned to look at him, but Alex only shook his head at her. When he did, she noticed a little silver cross around his neck swish back and forth, one of its points chipped off.

"This whole time you've been moping and writing numbers on your arm like a freak," Long said, his bloodshot eyes burning. "Do you think that's going to help anything? Do you think that's any better than giving up?"

"I think it's better than deluding yourself," Andrea said in a low voice. Alex gaped at her. *Hypocrite,* she thought. *He feels the same way.*

Long breathed sharply out his nose. "Tell you what I'm going to do. I'm going to read this textbook and find an answer and ignore you. You like numbers so much? This book is full of numbers." He held up the textbook and shook it at Andrea. "How about you look at these numbers and help us figure out how we got to be cannibalistic freaks of nature?"

Jaclyn shushed everyone, a shocking sound following Long's raised tone. "Stop yelling. Do you hear that?"

They were quiet long enough to hear yelling outside the classroom—Andrea thought the voice was counting down numbers, *three, two, one*—and then something exploded through the barricade in front of the classroom door. Chair legs splintered and flew around the room, clouding the remaining four in smoke. Andrea curled into the fetal position, her arms over her head.

Footsteps entered the classroom. "Hands in the air!" someone shouted.

Andrea looked up and, blinking against the smoke, saw Long lying on his side, blood in his open mouth. One of the chair legs had pierced through his back—through the heart. *Interesting,* Andrea thought. *Usually to kill us they aim for the brain.*

Someone pulled up Andrea by her arm, and her legs moved when the floor rushed under her. Alex yanked her to the closet. He shouted something and ran back toward the chaos, away from her.

She almost tripped over bodies on that side of the room before she stumbled into the closet. She shut the door behind her and, for a moment, was alone in the dark. She stepped forward, and her fingers grazed one of the walls. And that was it, just her and the little closet. *One,* she thought. *Oh God. One is a horrible number.*

But then the door opened behind her and Alex rushed in, dragging Jaclyn with him. Jaclyn fell to her knees, covering her face with her hands, just before the door shut. And then darkness enveloped them.

*T*able nine wanted more breadsticks. Long's Olive Garden apron swished back and forth when he brought the four-person family a basket of breadsticks. The mother and father gave Long grateful smiles when their two daughters dived into the basket. Long's stomach grumbled, but he smiled anyway and left. The man at table five wanted to look at the dessert menu.

*How many smiles until he could move to New York? How many more art classes at the community college until he had enough credits to transfer? Logically speaking, he needed money in order to achieve his dreams. Logically speaking, he was qualified to be a server at Olive Garden, but not much else. Do the math. He had to remind himself of the logic sometimes when his stomach turned over itself while carrying plate after plate of steaming hot food.*

*According to his parents, logically speaking, it was a good idea to visit his sister next week. Long gritted his teeth thinking about it. At least Jaclyn was taking a philosophy class. Maybe he could sit in that class, and maybe he'd even learn something about all this goddamned logic he was so intent on following.*

Andrea thought she would hear Jaclyn cry, but the closet was silent. Outside, she heard more Feds enter, their heavy boots thumping.

"I'm starving," Jaclyn said, her faint voice cracking the silence.

"There's nothing left to eat," Alex said. "We ate everything."

Jaclyn let out a harsh exhale that was probably meant to be a laugh. "Every*thing*. Nice way of putting it."

"Sorry," Alex muttered.

Andrea's head spun again, the darkness whirling around her. "I'm hungry, too." She barely recognized her own voice.

She reminded herself: three was a fantastic number. Three was everywhere. The Father, the Son, and the Holy Ghost. The past, the present, and the future. Beginning, middle, and end. She felt for her arm with the tip of the pen and tried to write a 3.

"Andrea," Alex's voice was hesitant, "what Long said. . . ." He trailed off and swallowed. "Why do you write numbers on your arm?"

Andrea capped the pen with a *click*, hesitating. "Just trying to keep track." She kept her voice light. "People are falling so fast it's hard to remember who's around and who's not."

Jaclyn whimpered.

"Do you really have to say it like that?" Alex said quietly. "Andrea, what's wrong with you?"

"Sorry, sorry," Andrea said, even though she wasn't. "I just . . . I mean, it's obvious that we're all going to die at this point, right? It's no surprise or anything."

"God," Alex sighed, "can you please shut up?"

Jaclyn's whimpering grew louder.

"I thought you were with me on this." Andrea's own voice was harsh in her ears. "Until I saw your stupid cross, anyway."

"My *stupid—*" Alex cut himself off. "I don't know what you thought, but you're wrong. I'm not with you if it means making a joke out of the fact that Long just died."

Jaclyn choked with sobs.

"I'm not making a joke out of it." Andrea huffed. "Is it really that unreasonable that I don't see the point of going on?" She tried to ignore Jaclyn when she cried harder. "It's like you said. We're dying anyway."

"I don't see the point, either," Alex said. "But that doesn't mean I want to die. And I'm certainly not counting down each dead body like it's fucking New Year's Eve."

"Shut up," Jaclyn screamed, her voice cracking. "Can you both please just *shut up?* God, I am *so hungry.*"

Andrea heard a scuffling of shoes and then the closet door swung open, the late afternoon sun flooding the classroom in a blinding glow. Jaclyn ran out and the door stayed open long enough for Andrea to see Jaclyn, her sharp nails outstretched, leap onto a Fed and scratch at his face. She and the Fed fell, and the room outside erupted into screams and gunshots and spurting that made Andrea's head spin. Then the door closed, and they returned to darkness and the dead silence of the closet.

*J aclyn was the first to know something was wrong.*

*She knew long before the six of them—Professor Hunter and five of his students—had gone out and devoured every living being on campus to quench their fresh hunger.*

*She knew before her professor attacked all fifteen students in the class, leaving ten dead and five turned into the same kind of monster as he was with the same horrible hungers.*

*She knew before he locked the door of the classroom, grabbed the back of a student's shirt, and sunk his teeth into the back of the poor sophomore's neck, tearing out a chunk of flesh.*

*She knew before he started writing the definition of* epistemology *on the board (*the theory of knowledge, *Jaclyn had copied in her notes in a cursive script).*

*She knew before the beginning of class when he announced blithely that he was starving and couldn't wait until class ended so he could get lunch.* "So let's get started, shall we?"

*She knew even before she volunteered at the hospital that morning when one of the nurses told her about a strange case they'd gotten in the middle of the night: a woman with a bite mark on her arm dropping dead after devouring her husband's shoulder.*

*No, she knew something was wrong when Long called her the previous day, asking tersely if he could sit in on her philosophy class. Because Jaclyn knew that every time she and Long were together, something always went wrong.*

Hours passed, and Andrea and Alex said nothing. Andrea didn't know how Alex felt, but she wasn't sure if she could take any more of the spinning, so they sat while the world outside fell into chaos.

Finally, Alex stood and slowly opened the door. The room stung with the yellow light of streetlights, beams falling through the blinds and into the dark classroom. Each beam lit up a broken chair leg, a spatter of blood on the floor, Long's mouth full of dried blood, the lifeless face of a Fed, Jaclyn's bloodstained blouse, the dust from the explosion spinning in the air. Andrea saw where Jaclyn had been shot in the back of the head, a small pool of dark blood matting her blonde hair. There was no life in the room.

Alex gingerly walked into the classroom. He scanned the room, his face lit up by the streetlight. He squinted against it and turned to look at Andrea, who still stood just inside the closet doorway. "Now what do we do?" His voice echoed around the classroom.

"Don't know," Andrea murmured. To her left, she saw Ari, where they'd left her, covered in Alex's and Long's jackets, and she edged farther into the closet. Her hands balled into fists, but there was nothing in them, and she realized what she was missing. "My pen. Where's my pen?" She looked around the closet, seeing nothing. "Shit, I think I dropped it in here."

Alex stared at her and shook his head. "Of all the things to worry about right now."

Andrea wanted to tell him that two was maybe the best number there was. It was full of opposites: true and false, Heaven and Hell, yin and yang, good and evil, life and death. Two was a balance. Two was perfection.

Instead, she got down on her hands and knees and crawled blindly through the closet, looking for the pen, and asked Alex, "You understand sentimental value, don't you?" Her fingers slid along the cool dark floor. Nothing. "That's why you still have that chipped cross."

Alex didn't respond for a moment. "Yeah, I guess you're right. It was my grandfather's. It's . . . just sentimental."

The only sound was Andrea scuffling along the closet floor like some kind of wild animal.

"Can I tell you something?" Alex finally asked.

Andrea looked up from the dark closet to his face yellow with streetlight. She squinted. "What?"

He stared at his hands, gently wiggling the stump of his pointer finger. "I've read books in every single classroom we've hidden in. Ever since this started, ever since we were in Professor Hunter's class a week ago, I've been reading books. I just read today that mammals have a protein named after Sonic the Hedgehog. I read last night, when we were hiding in the history department, that Franz Ferdinand's wife was also killed on the day he was assassinated, and she died ten minutes before he did, and Franz's last words were begging his wife not to die. And a few days before that, before the Feds came to get us and I was in the music building, surrounded by dead people that I didn't remember killing, I read that Sergei Rachmaninoff's hands were gigantic, and that pianists have gone insane trying to play some of his songs because their hands aren't big enough to play his music."

Andrea blinked. "So?"

He sighed. "So you can't exactly write any of that down on your arm, can you?"

Andrea felt sick in her hollow chest. "I said the pen was sentimental."

"It's not sentimental, Andrea. I can tell. You're not the sentimental type."

"You don't get it," she said, her head spinning. "I need the numbers, okay? I need them. I need them or else what's the point? I mean, there's no point." She shook her head. "There's no point to any of this. We're all going to die and that's fine; that's great, actually. I don't care. Okay? I don't care. I don't care if I die. But the day I have to write a 1 on my arm is the day that everything's really gone to shit."

Alex's eyes softened. "Andrea."

"Just don't die, okay? Please don't die. I know we're not great friends or anything but you're the only one left who gets it, so please don't die, okay? I don't want to write a 1."

There was a thump from somewhere in the room, and Alex turned toward it, but the streetlight didn't touch the patch of darkness from where the noise came.

"Alex," Andrea said, frozen. "Alex, come into the closet."

He didn't. "Who's there?" he called.

"Alex, get in the fucking closet. Get in the closet or I'm going out there with you."

Before Andrea could move, a bullet cut through the darkness and the streetlights and into Alex's brain. He stumbled, arms flailing, and collapsed to his knees. Andrea thought she could see the moment his brain shut off forever, when his head lolled to the side and he fell in a pile on the floor. *Why do they have to shoot us in the head to kill us? That was the best part of him. Did they have to kill that?*

Andrea sat in the closet, not bothering to close the door, and watched a shadowy figure walk through the classroom. His helmet was illuminated, and the barrel of his gun pointed at her. She closed her eyes and waited.

Then his voice, gravelly: "You're the last one. They told us not to kill the last one."

Andrea opened her eyes and the yellow light stung. "What?"

"Trust me, sweetheart," he said, lowering his gun, "as much as I'd like to, they want to keep you alive for testing."

*A*lex *wrote out one flashcard for* aesthetics *and one for* metaphysics. *He tapped absentmindedly on the table with a finger that Professor Hunter would eat later in the semester. Across from him, Andrea sleepily scanned their philosophy textbook. They sat in a café off campus where Alex liked to do his homework.*

*"Okay, that's all of them," Alex said, shuffling the flashcards and holding them up for Andrea, one after the other. She answered tiredly, fine with some of the definitions and struggling over the others.*

*"Metaphysics," she said. "A branch of philosophy that has to do with . . . the fundamental nature of being and stuff."*

*"Well put," he said, pulling out the next one.*

*"Aesthetics," she said, narrowing her eyes. "Um. When you think everything is pretty? Or something?"*

*"A branch of philosophy dealing with the nature of art, beauty, and taste," Alex told her, reading off the back of the card.*

*"Close enough," Andrea said, biting into her scone.*

*"You can't write 'when you think everything is pretty' on the test if aesthetics comes up," Alex said.*

*Andrea swallowed. "Whatever. It's kind of a superficial branch of philosophy, anyway."*

*"What's superficial about beauty?"*

*"All you're doing is analyzing why stuff is pretty," Andrea said. "Not, 'Who are we?' or 'What is reality?' but, like, 'Why do I think this necklace is pretty?'"*

*"Not just necklaces." Alex leaned in toward her, suddenly feeling the beating of his heart. "It has to do with why you like to read certain books or why you like to watch certain movies. What people find beautiful says a lot about society and about who they are." He smiled at her. "Why do you think necklaces are pretty?"*

*Andrea shrugged. "I don't really care all that much about necklaces."*

*A*ndrea is a medical fascination. The doctors thought she would die as soon as she got to the lab. But she lives, and strangers prod and poke and drain and inspect her day after day.

Time passes, and she lives long enough to spy a pen in a doctor's office, on a stack of papers she knows contain data about her. It's not her whiteboard marker. Just a ballpoint pen, not great for writing on skin. But it'll do. If she doesn't struggle, if she obeys, they'll trust her and let her use a pen. Eventually.

More time passes, and she's been there long enough they don't feel the need to strap her to the bed. It has been weeks, maybe months. Andrea doesn't really care. Those aren't the numbers she's interested in keeping track of.

One day, she's in a doctor's office, and the doctor walks out of the office to get a medical instrument, leaving Andrea alone with his pen. She gets off the bed, takes the pen sitting on the pile of paper, and writes a belated 2 and a 1 on her arm. The 5, 4, and 3 are completely gone.

She is one.

Andrea lies back on the bed and curls into the fetal position and shuts her eyes. She was never supposed to be one, not for this long. There's no point to it.

The doctors tell her there's a point. They say her samples could be used to invent a cure before this disease spreads too far. But Andrea is in her own mind, not in the minds of people being saved; not in the minds of these doctors believing they're doing the right thing; not in the dead minds of her dead classmates. She's only in her own mind.

And in her own mind, she knows one is a horrible number. She wants to be zero.

# THE BOATS
## Robb T. White

Graciela was a shy girl who clung to her mother. They had made the trip from Guatemala three years previously by traversing a thousand miles of rainforest and desert, passing hostile villages where locals greeted them with stones in case they lingered to beg for food. The worst of the journey had been the final crossing into El Norte.

The coyotes working for the Sinaloa Cartel had packed twenty-nine of them into an empty oil tank truck in broiling heat in Juárez Valley, across the border from Texas. By the time they were released, twelve had died in that steel oven; the rest were dehydrated and barely able to walk. Graciela's mother survived only three months after they arrived. She had been too weak to be hired as a motel maid, which had been her plan to support Graciela once they were safely across the border.

Because she was only twelve at the time of her mother's death, Graciela was hustled from one relative to the other. First, an aunt in San Antonio rescued her from the streets when a kindly stranger made a call to a distant cousin in Matamoros. Graciela stayed with her aunt and her large family for six months and then, in the middle of the night, was hurriedly dressed and shipped north to her father's cousin in Fredericksburg. Eighteen months later, when ICE was going through town rounding up illegals, she was driven to yet another relative in Kerrville.

Graciela remembered being carsick because of the endless up-and-down, winding highway. By then, she was told to call herself

Gracie. Her halting English, the blue-black Indian hair of her genetic heritage, eyes so dark the irises seemed to disappear—all of it kept her from fitting in.

When she turned fifteen, she was enrolled in her seventh school; her loneliness was a physical anguish that squeezed her insides. She inserted a towel between her teeth to keep her sobs from waking up the family. They were kind enough, but nothing could replace her mother, who had been buried in a potter's field in a border town whose name she couldn't recall. Graciela created a fantasy that her mother was buried in the hill country around Fredericksburg, with its bluebonnets and brilliant wildflowers and cedars. As time passed, she added more details: fence posts weathered gray near pastures, where mesquite lay in profusion and giant oaks spread their arms over spring-fed creeks.

When Juanita Rivera sat beside her at lunch one day, Graciela looked about nervously, expecting the brash and popular girl to mock her as other girls had done for her failure to speak good English. Her grades were dismal, not because she wasn't intelligent, for she was possessed of a vibrant imagination, but because every subject depended on a fluency she struggled to acquire. The teachers were unwilling to hold her back for a reason they never told her: she was developing physically at a much faster pace than other girls. She was sent home at the start of the year, in fact, because her breasts strained against the hand-me-down blouse.

Juanita, however, surprised Graciela with her friendliness. When Graciela didn't understand references to popular music or a TV show or a Hollywood celebrity, the other girl would patiently explain it. She never laughed at her shyness; instead, she complimented Graciela on her stunningly dark eyes and lovely hair.

Once, when Juanita walked her to the bus, she reached out and felt Graciela's breast. "Shit, girl, those tits are real!"

Graciela's face burned with a mix of shame and pride. She couldn't speak the whole time Juanita danced around her, cupping her own small breasts in comparison and laughing: "Hell, Gracie, you should flaunt those big girls of yours."

That was the first night Graciela hadn't cried for her mother.

Her life improved with Juanita's friendship, and soon she wasn't ignored by the other girls. Even the teachers showed more patience though most continued to talk down to her; several looked down on "Mexicans" despite the fact the entire faculty was Mexican-American.

Soon Juanita was giving her clothes. Graciela refused until Juanita made it plain she would be offended if she kept refusing. Graciela, terrified to lose the friendship of the only person her age who had ever befriended her, gradually relented and went to school in Juanita's castoffs, each trendier than her best outfits.

Graciela was wary of the boys who gathered around Juanita. Juanita was older than her years, and her sexual references often went over Graciela's head or made her deeply uncomfortable. When they were together or with other girls, Juanita kept the spicier parts of her vocabulary at bay, but when boys came around, it was a different story. Sexual double entendre was inevitable, and often the older boys used coarse language. Graciela's mother would not approve of Juanita.

Juanita's father owned three motels in town, one of which was downtown in El Centro. The motel was populated with transients, winos, drug dealers, and addicts.

One Monday after third period, Juanita caught Graciela at her locker and said her father was willing to pay them eight dollars an hour to be motel maids.

"C'mon, Gracie," Juanita pleaded, "don't pussy out on me. I already told him yes."

Graciela wasn't sure her family (school authorities listed them as her godparents) would agree, but Juanita said she'd drop by that evening after supper and sweet talk them into agreeing. Besides, the job was on weekends, and what about the money they'd have to spend?

"Leave it to me, babe," Juanita promised. "I know how to get my way."

Graciela agreed, impressed how Juanita could charm anyone.

When Juanita arrived that night, Graciela's family, who were devout Catholics, spoke broken English since Graciela had told them Juanita didn't speak Spanish, and Graciela wisely omitted the plethora of curse words her friend had access to.

Friday that week, Graciela rode the bus downtown and walked a couple blocks to The Grand Hotel. She expected to see a pastel-colored motel like the ones on the highway, but this was a three-storey, decrepit, weather-beaten building with cardboard taped over missing window panes. The glass plate window facing the street was grimy and made a joke of the fancy gilt lettering of the hotel's name.

When she entered the hotel, two old men with long beards were sitting in plastic chairs, reading magazines, and barely glanced at her. A man wearing thick glasses looked her over from behind the curved wooden desk but didn't say anything when she approached.

"I'm Juanita's friend," she said. "I'm supposed to meet her here."

"Third floor, room three-oh-four," he said and went back to his magazine.

She headed for the elevator until she saw an "Out of Order" sign.

The place stank of disinfectant and stale cooking odors. The carpeting on the third floor was nasty; every few feet someone had crushed out a cigarette. She hesitated and almost turned around but chided herself for "pridefulness," a church word, for thinking her friend's place wasn't good enough for her. Besides, she'd be working side-by-side with Juanita, the owner's daughter. He'd never allow his child to work here if anything was wrong.

She breathed deeply and knocked.

The balding, middle-aged Mexican-American who opened the door wore a white long-sleeved shirt rolled up to his forearms. A gold bracelet shone from one wrist and a large gold watch on the other.

"You Juanita's friend?"

"Yes," she said.

"She not here yet," he said. "Come in."

The room was depressing, with a small iron-framed bed, a single lamp on a night table, and an old dresser with a mirror opposite the bed.

"You want to sit?"

"No, thank you, sir," she said.

"Call me Joe."

She wished Juanita would hurry so they could start. Being in a hotel room with a strange man, even if he was her friend's father, made her uncomfortable. She felt the same about the assistant principal, Mister Herrera, who always stared at her chest.

"Like a drink—what's your name?"

"No, no, sir. Graciela," she said. Being offered a drink made her stomach flutter.

"Here," he insisted, "have one. Just a little to take the edge off." He held out a tumbler holding amber liquid.

Dark-complexioned though she was, she knew her face flushed crimson. She turned around and had one hand almost on the doorknob. "I'll—I'll wait for Juanita in the lobby."

She never made it. Joe grabbed her thick hair and yanked her backwards to the floor. He straddled her chest, backhanding her face with hard slaps until she tasted blood.

When he stood, she thought it was a bizarre accident. Some incredible mistake that must have an explanation. Her brain couldn't process what had happened. She struggled to her feet. Her eyes watered from the slaps, and her cheeks burned with fire. She sensed he waited behind her. She tottered toward the door.

The punch to her liver dropped her to the floor again, and this time, she couldn't breathe or see through a red-hot sheet of pain.

When she recovered her senses, she believed she was waking up from a nightmare. Time had vanished—but, no, he stood at the door, whispering to someone. Joe had stripped to underwear and socks, and thick black hair grew on his back in a figure-eight pattern. She remained on the bed. Terror again swept over her. She reached down to her pudenda, which was slick, and sharp stabs of pain welled up from her lower abdomen. She touched her vagina and brought away bloody fingers.

She screamed.

In a split-second, he was leaning over her, his fist balled for a strike.

"Yell one word, *puta* bitch, and I'll kill you!"

His spittle flecked her face. She cried.

He grabbed her chin in his hand and squeezed her jaw until she thought it would crack.

"Don't say anything," he said. "This is how you're going to earn your money. I'll be standing right outside the door. If I hear you speak, I'll come in here and I'll go to work on your face."

He produced a thin-bladed knife and turned it back and forth in front of her face. "Just do what you're made for, bitch. I'll have you and your whole goddam family kicked out, *los sin papeles*. Juanita says you're a stuck-up bitch. We gonna change that right now."

The first man through the door wore cowboy boots and reeked of a ferocious body odor. He said nothing to her but stripped beside the bed, climbed on top of her, and forced himself inside.

Much later, Gracelia's memory protected her from the worst of it, but she remembered enough that she hid in a closet for weeks afterward, where she covered herself and usually remained during the day. She stopped going to school. Her godparents didn't know what to do with her and finally decided to leave her alone. They left out food at night. She crept into the kitchen like a scavenging animal and ate some of what they left for her. She had no appetite, and her weight dropped. Urination and swallowing became painful. They took her to a free clinic, where she was diagnosed with chlamydia of the genitals and gonorrhoea of the throat.

Over the next few weeks, she began to recover her strength. The first day she left the house, she saw a man crossing the street who had been "one of them." A white-hot flame burned inside her and dictated what she did next. Before he got into his car, she ran at him, screaming and spitting, "You ruined my life!"

She prayed every night to the Virgin Mary, but the Blessed Mother didn't answer. One afternoon, Juanita passed by her house with several girls from school. When Juanita pointed at the house, they laughed.

Graciela took three months to prepare. She worked every night in her godfather's garage, making two boats. He was a good carpenter, and he showed her how to plane wood and how to use the circular saw and other tools. Her godparents never asked her about the STDs; they were humble, shy people with modest jobs as dishwasher and landscaper. They assumed woodworking was her way of healing herself. In a way, they were right.

The hard part was still to come.

Juanita's father was a fanatical Sunday golfer. One of the neighborhood boys, Miggy, was a caddie at the club. Graciela knew Miggy liked her, for he'd often asked her out on dates, which she'd always refused.

She convinced Miggy to sneak her in the club through the caddies' clubhouse, and she scanned the golf course through the window.

"What you lookin' for, Gracie?"

"Which holes are the toughest on the course?"

Miggy said it was the seventeenth, known as "the putters' graveyard" because of the balls that rolled off the high-pitched slope of the putting green and wound up in the putrid muck of the mangrove swamp bordering the green.

"Show me," she said, and they walked across the course to the seventeenth green. She knelt and studied the swamp while Miggy stood on the manicured green, looking down at her. The marsh buzzed with insect life. Dragonflies with iridescent wings flew in and out of a brace of cattails.

That Sunday near sunset, while Juanita's father was lining up a birdie putt, Graciela came up on his blind side and stepped in front of him. He recognized her too late. She stuck the Taser that Miggy had given her under his chin. The spark crackled and made him dance like a puppet with its strings cut. He flopped on the green, one hand hitting the flagstick so hard the flag flew off.

He was heavy but she was stronger than ever. Most of her weight had returned, and thanks to her godfather's power tools, she had doubled her arm strength.

She duct-taped his mouth and dragged him by his feet down to the swamp's edge. She recovered one the ropes she'd hidden and pulled in the first boat. Miggy had transported the boats in his van and hauled them to the swamp in one of the club's carts. She'd refused to tell him what the boats were for.

She removed one of the gunwales from its grooved channel and managed to get an arm, then a leg, and finally the rest of the man's bulk rolled onto the concave boat. She fitted the slender gunwale back in place; the boats she had designed were little more than plywood boards with removable sides. She fastened belts from Goodwill to his hands and feet. Once secure to the boat's bottom, she used a serrated kitchen knife to tear the clothing from beneath him. She pocketed his car keys and cell phone and then tossed his clothing, precious golf clubs, and golf bag into the swamp.

Graciela prayed to the Virgin for the strength to finish. From a submerged plastic baggie weighted down in the mud, she drew out a large bottle of honey and smeared it over his face, chest, arms, and legs. She couldn't bear to touch his genitals, so she tilted the bottle over his crotch and watched honey ooze out.

She gripped the rope and stepped into the filthy water, pulling her human cargo behind her through the reeds until she was thigh deep in the water. She pushed the boat past her and watched it float slowly to the middle of the marsh. From the shoreline, he would be invisible. Gagged, he wouldn't be heard by golfers putting on the seventeenth.

She hopped into the golf cart and headed back to the clubhouse, where Miggy waited.

"I ain't gonna ask what you did out there all this time, Gracie," he said and walked away.

She looked up Juanita in her father's cell directory and texted her to meet him at the seventeenth green to collect her surprise birthday gift. "Come alone, baby girl," Graciela added, using his term of endearment.

Juanita would be expecting to collect a shiny set of car keys inside the cup of the seventeenth green. She had repeatedly told Graciela that her father promised her a Mazda MX-5 convertible on her seventeenth birthday.

An hour later, with darkness descending and the golfers gone, Juanita knelt over the cup hole, feeling around for her long-promised keys. Graciela, silent as a big cat at a jungle watering hole, crept up behind her with the Taser. For Juanita, as well, recognition came too late.

"What—what are you doing here, cunt?"

The smack of the Taser against Juanita's neck was more satisfying than Graciela had hoped. Juanita's body, stripped and taped, was a featherweight compared to her beer-bellied father.

Graciela ripped the duct tape off Juanita's face when she came to. Groaning but still dazed, Juanita focused on Graciela's face.

"Your treachery hurt me more than those men did, Juanita," Graciela said.

Before Juanita could scream, Graciela replaced the tape over her mouth and then held the other girl's chin.

"Look at me," Graciela said. "See this? It's going in your eyes, your ears, your mouth, and most of all, down there." She teased a line with her fingernail over Juanita's trimmed pubic ruff. "But I'll show you some mercy. Your father, that pig, will be floating out there with you. You won't see him, but he'll be there with his eyes wide open."

Juanita's eyes flashed and tears formed.

"Pretty soon, insects will come," Graciela said. "The flies, mosquitoes, the wasps—for the honey, you see."

More and more insects would be drawn by the smell. They'd soon burrow under Juanita's and her father's flesh to lay their eggs. Exposed under the burning sun, lying in their urine and feces, itching from the bites, and starving and dehydrated, their minds would become unhinged in a couple of days. The bites would turn gangrenous, and septic shock would eventually kill them. Graciela had seen it in her mind a thousand times since that day those men had lined up outside the door.

If the current ninety-degree heat continued, she would have to sneak back to give Juanita and her father water so they didn't die of dehydration too soon.

Graciela had numbed herself with the hardest part of the father's "boat," which had involved using an eyelash curler and a razor to remove his eyelids so that his eyeballs would bear the full brunt of the unrelenting sun.

She returned every night for three days. The TV stations and the paper had reported that Texas EquuSearch would help with the search for the missing father and daughter.

The father went first. The smell wafting from his boat nearly gagged Graciela even though she held a rag over her mouth when she waded out with a bottle of water. He was the color of eggplant, and one end of the tape had been chewed off. His partly open mouth gushed with maggots. Juanita's blackened face was lumpy and distorted so badly that her eyes, nose, mouth, and ears were unrecognizable. Columns of descending insects hovered, their feasting disturbed by Graciela's presence.

Graciela waded back to shore, her mind floating back to the boats, pushing water aside with each hand like a black-eyed sea goddess emerging from dark waters.

# PAYBACKS
## Leslie Muzingo

**C**harlie sat cross-legged in the back of the van. Comfortable in leather leggings and buckskin tunic, and refreshed by the mountain air, he couldn't help but feel the call of his ancestors until the signs directing them to Donner Pass reminded him why he was there in the first place. He recalled the conversation he'd had with Dr. Phil Stein, Professor of Anthropology. . . .

**"S**o how much debt do I have left to work off from a couple of lousy card games?" Charlie asked Stein. He saw Stein's eyes light up with evil intent, and then, as if the spark was blown out, the look in Stein's eyes was replaced with false innocence.

"Only a couple more of these studies. But you love doing them, don't you?" Stein clapped his arm over Charlie's shoulder and pulled him close as if trying to include him in something. Charlie didn't understand what was going on, but he understood enough to know he didn't want to be involved any longer than what was necessary to pay off his debt.

"Maybe I would if I understood what you were doing. Explain it again." Charlie pulled away from Stein. He hated admitting that none of this made any sense, but he didn't want to get tricked into doing something wrong. Although they'd done what Stein called "a prank" twice, both times involving only one student, Charlie didn't trust Stein not to implicate him in a later scheme and stick him with all the blame.

How happy Stein had seemed at the prospect of having an audience. Whenever Charlie had asked the man a question, Stein would get puffed up, stand tall, and clear his throat before he'd respond. It seemed to Charlie that Stein must love being a professor and standing in front of a big class and talking because he certainly loved making a show out of explaining things.

Stein took his pencil from his pocket and waved it in the air while answering Charlie's question. Stein looked as if he was using it like a pointer except, of course, there wasn't anything for Stein to point at. Charlie felt like a class of one when Stein began every lecture with "It is a psychological anthropological study." That last time, Stein had added: "We are studying the interaction of cultural and mental processes under stress. Stress makes people act in all sorts of interesting ways. But we need people who are similar or it isn't a valid study. By taking people who were raised and educated in approximately the same way and putting them in an extremely—"

Charlie breathed in the crisp air and pushed the thoughts behind him. How could the others be so drowsy? He found the mountain air invigorating.

Finally, Dr. Stein broke the silence. "I've planned a fun surprise for everyone. I know you're going to love it. I've made arrangements for us to camp at the Donner Pass campground."

Two of the students, Pete and Sara, barely opened their eyes at the news. Travis looked ready to hyperventilate. The boy squirmed in his seat. With shaking hands, he took a pill and began biting his cuticles down to blood. Suddenly he tapped Dr. Stein's shoulder like a woodpecker pecking on a dead tree.

"Yes, Travis?" Dr. Stein asked without taking his eyes off the road.

"Doctor Stein! Doctor Stein! We can't camp at Donner Pass tonight. It's against the rules to camp there after October first, so we can't camp there."

Charlie felt the vibrations from Travis' sigh of relief.

Dr. Stein, at that minute, was pulling into the deserted campground. Stopping the van, he turned around in his seat and looked at Travis. "Calm down, my boy. I got us special permission. We are not ordinary campers—we are anthropologists! And don't we have Injun Charlie with us, a bona fide Ute Indian guide? Now onward to finding a good place to set up camp." Dr. Stein turned back to the wheel, whistling while he drove.

Once parked, Stein barked orders to the students about how to set up camp. Charlie had his own work in the woods, so he left the group to handle the campsite. He wasn't far away, though, and heard Stein telling the students where to put the sleeping bags and gear. From his vantage point, Charlie saw Sara slide over to Stein while the young men made camp. Charlie found the only problem with superb vision was seeing things he wished he hadn't. This time, he saw Dr. Stein fondle Sara's behind. From what Charlie could tell, Sara stiffened but gave Stein a mask-like smile of encouragement. Charlie turned his back and continued his work. He'd seen more than enough.

Soon he heard Stein say, "It's almost dark, and we need firewood. If we separate, we can quickly gather enough. Come on, team, let's go."

Charlie watched the students leave. Then he went back to his work.

While he was in the woods, he came upon Pete. Charlie stood by a tree and watched. Although the most physically able of Dr. Stein's students, Pete was talking on the phone instead of gathering wood.

"Doctor Prescott? Can you hear me? NOW CAN YOU HEAR ME? Lousy coverage here. Listen, I HEAR YOU NEED A RESEARCH ASSISTANT. NO, I'M SURE DOCTOR STEIN DOESN'T NEED ME ANYMORE. REALLY. Hello? HELLO? ARE YOU THERE, DOCTOR PRESCOTT? Goddammit!" Pete flipped his phone shut and turned. "What do you want, injun?"

Charlie walked away. As a member of The People, he knew better than wasting his time with boys who would never be men.

Soon he came upon Sara, who had gathered a large stack of wood. He looked at the wood and then at Sara. "How you get the pile to camp?"

"Why—" She looked at him expectantly.

"It not so easy to do yourself what you expect others to do for you." He left Sara with her mouth open. He had no time for blondes.

Charlie's work was almost complete when he found Travis stuffing a bag with wood. "I d-don't want us to run out," the young man said with a slight stutter. "The fire keeps animals away, isn't t-that right?"

Charlie nodded.

"My grandmother used to tell stories about animals coming after me at night. I just hate the d-dark."

Charlie saw a nice hunk of wood Travis had missed, so he reached down and handed it to him.

"Thanks." Travis pushed his glasses back up his nose with a quivering finger.

Charlie finished his task and returned to the campsite, where he found Dr. Stein covered in blood. Stein moaned. Blood had pooled next to the man. Charlie knew to act fast. He grabbed the first bag he saw, opened it, took out a shirt, and ripped it into strips.

He found it odd that at certain crucial times of his life he noticed the little things—always something unimportant that caught his attention. This time he heard the students laughing far away, down by the lake, while he ripped fabric for the tourniquet. Overhead, a male bluebird sang a gay autumn song. Time briefly stood still during the laughter and song, and he felt the rip of fabric beneath his fingers.

Then the spell was broken, and he returned to everyday madness.

By the time the students arrived, he was tying the tourniquet.

"What did you do to my shirt, you son-of-a-bitch?" Pete exclaimed. The boy stepped toward Charlie as if he might try to fight him. Charlie managed to hold back his laughter.

"Oh, my God, what happened to Doctor Stein," Travis cried.

Charlie had to give Travis credit. At least he saw past the ripped shirt and noticed his professor covered in blood.

Sara gulped before asking, "Was it a bear?"

"No bear," Charlie grunted without looking up. "Done with a knife."

A three count of silence. Then Travis whispered, "But who?"

Charlie finished tying the tourniquet before he faced three pairs of eyes staring at him. "Ask him." Charlie moved so Dr. Stein could see all three students. "Who did this?"

Stein moaned. He lifted his arm and pointed one finger at the students who stood grouped together. His arm then dropped weakly to his side.

"He's crazy," Pete exclaimed. "We were gathering wood. None of us could have possibly done this to him."

Charlie pushed down the van's back seats and spread out the sleeping bags. "You weren't gathering wood. You were quitting him." Charlie pointed to Dr. Stein.

You don't think Pete—" Sara said.

"Maybe you. Doctor liked to touch you. You didn't like it. Maybe you stopped him."

Charlie picked up Dr. Stein as if he were a precious baby and placed him in the van.

"Don't talk to a lady like that," Travis said.

Charlie grabbed the last sleeping bag and covered Stein, tucking him in. "Or maybe you. You scared to be here. Very scared." Charlie got in the van and started the engine. "I take him to hospital. Then I get sheriff."

"But what about bears?" Sara cried.

"Bears fat now, not hungry for man. You have the gun with one bullet. Shoot in the air and you scare off the bear." Without another word, Charlie drove away.

Just then it began to snow.

***

Stein exited the bathroom, drying himself off with a towel. "Damn deer blood really stinks."

Nate Prescott, one of Stein's fellow professors, handed Stein a bourbon and water. "Here, Phil. Suck your drink and you'll feel better."

Stein settled into a chair. "Hope we can rewind it, Charlie, because—"

The Indian's chin went up. "The name is Charles."

Stein laughed. "Really? Okay, if that's what you want. So, can we rewind it?"

Charlie popped some peanuts into his mouth. "No problem. I had plenty of time to set the cameras and microphones while you had them make camp."

"So, rewind it, *Charles*."

Charlie ignored the sarcasm and rewound the recording.

"Stop there!" Stein cried. "I don't need it further back than that. Let's watch."

*"Fucking great tour guide you turned out to be," Pete screamed at the departing vehicle. He turned, red-faced, to the others who were staring at him. "Don't you see? That mother-fucker is the one who hurt Stein. He's probably taking him somewhere to kill him off and here we stood like fools and let it happen."*

*"Pete, no!" Sara said. "Doctor Stein told me more than once how much he trusted Charlie."*

*Pete rolled his eyes. "I bet he did. Was that before you got in bed with him or after?"*

*"How dare you!"*

*Travis stepped between them. "Pete, I'm not going to let you insult her."*

*"What are you going to do about it? Charlie had at least one thing right, Travis. You are a big fucking pussy!"*

*Sara jumped between the young men. "Let's just calm down and wait till the sheriff gets here."*

*Travis suddenly looked pained. "He took all of the sleeping bags. And it's snowing."*

*"Pussy."*

*"It's snowing!"*

*"Meow."*

*"Stop," Sara screamed.*

*"It's snowing," Travis cried.*

*"So, go call your grandma."*

*"Don't you talk about my grandmother!"*

*Sara tried again to step between the young men. "Stop it!"*

*"Like I'd listen to a slut like you." Pete turned away.*

*"Don't you call her that!"*
*Pete turned back. "Grandma pussy, just shut the fuck up!"*
*Travis' hands began to shake uncontrollably.*

The professors watched the recording over and over. They laughed harder every time they watched it, each time toasting to their own genius and success.

Charlie had to know one thing. "Will they graduate?"

"Got to graduate Pete. His family is alums," Prescott said as he drained his glass for the fifth time.

Charlie laughed. "So grad school is just who you know, is it?"

"Sometimes, but he'll never get his Ph.D.," Stein remarked. "No other school will have him."

"Speaking of pretending, what about Sara?" Prescott asked while he poured Stein and himself another drink.

"It used to be that young girls knew to at least pretend they liked it," Stein said with a shake of his head. "But of course, she'll graduate. We don't want a lawsuit, after all."

"And Travis? He's the smartest, right?" Charlie asked.

Stein reached over and turned up the sound on the monitor.

A few minutes of silence passed while the men watched the recording.

"I see," Charlie said.

"You never know which one will grab the gun," Stein said, his eyes getting heavy.

"The best part is when they find out the gun isn't loaded. My God, this is hysterical." Prescott laughed, slapping his knee in slow motion.

Stein chuckled. "It wasn't who I thought it would be, that's for sure."

The two professors had another drink, and then another. They played the recording repeatedly. Finally, Charlie got up and made himself another drink. "You study people who are educated in approximately the same way, huh? You know, you two should both get to go sometime. We could find some way of making it work."

Prescott and Stein smiled at Charlie through liquor-laden eyes. Charlie smiled back. He brought the bottle to them and topped their drinks. "*Maybe i*nstead of having the students get worked up over some unknown assailant, they could instead witness one of you trying to off the other one. You two have an argument, and one of you grabs the gun. What do you think?" He stepped away and set the bottle back on the counter.

The professors nodded in agreement.

"Sounds fascinating," Stein remarked to his drink.

"Fascinating," Prescott repeated.

"Shall I set it up?" Charlie asked.

"Yes, yes, you do that," the men murmured.

"Who will be the aggressor and who the victim?" Charlie reached for the bottle and topped off his drink.

"Oh, I should get to do the shooting—" Prescott was cut off by a look from Stein. "Except this is your baby, Stein."

Stein showed his satisfaction with a smug smile. Holding out his glass to Charlie for a refill, he replied, "I'd let you go first except you never know about these things. As the person in charge, I should take the risks with the students."

Charlie accepted the glass and turned to refill Stein's drink. "There won't be any risks," he said loudly for both professors to hear. Then, softly to himself, "Except maybe this time the gun will be loaded."

# FEEDING STRAYS
## Monique Youzwa

The first time I saw the little girl she was crouched near the wall below the scuffed, barred windows of a pawn shop, among a few dented garbage cans. Her dirty clothes and dark, stringy hair almost blended into the shadows, but the glare of a streetlight shone in her wide, staring eyes. I stopped, glancing around to see if her parents were nearby, but the filth that covered her face and the shabby nature of her clothes screamed homeless and orphan. I stepped closer, and her gaze shifted from the crowded restaurant across the street to me. She didn't blink, only stared at me, her young face lined with dirt, her eyes filled with a haunting wisdom far beyond her years.

"Are you all right, sweetie?" I crouched, my eyes even with hers. They followed me down, locked on mine, the only movement she made. "Where is your family? Your mother?"

There was no answer from the girl, and her silence, her stillness, frightened me almost as much as her blank yet somehow knowing stare. I considered standing, turning around, and walking as quickly away from her as I could, but she was a child alone on the street. She needed help, and I couldn't leave her.

While I considered options, her eyes shifted away from me. It was like a weight lifted from my shoulders, no longer having to return her gaze without flinching away. She stared over my shoulder, and I glanced back to see what had caught her attention.

An older, well-dressed couple had come out of the restaurant. They strolled along the sidewalk, the woman's hand draped over the man's folded arm, a takeout bag swinging at her side. I peered at the little girl again and watched her eyes while she followed the couple. The tip of her tongue slipped out, touching her dry, dirty lips.

"Are you hungry?"

Her eyes darted back to me.

"I can get you some food, if you'd like."

The girl didn't move or answer but continued to stare with those glassy eyes.

"Stay here," I said and backed away from her. I checked to be sure the street was clear of cars and darted across to the restaurant.

The restaurant was busy. The hostess barely looked at me when she informed me there would be at least an hour's wait for a table. I grabbed a menu off the podium she reigned over. She started to scold me, but I cut her off, telling her my order was to go, and that if she couldn't take it herself, to send over someone who could. She stormed away, speaking to an older man in a rather expensive-looking suit who was obviously not a waitress.

"Can I help you, miss?" he asked, his teeth shining in the dim lighting.

"I need to place a takeout order." I scanned the menu, searching for something a little girl would eat. I didn't know very much about children, having had none myself, but I didn't think any pasta other than mac and cheese would do. Maybe a sandwich?

"We don't do takeout, miss. If you'd like a table—"

"It's not for me. It's for a little girl. I'm pretty sure she's homeless and starving. I want to get her some food until I can call the police, or a social worker, or someone who can help her."

"Miss, there are a lot of people here ahead of you who will not be happy to be pushed aside so you can have your meal first." He gestured to the dozen or so people standing clustered in the small alcove near the door. They were talking amongst themselves, barely even looking at us.

"I told you, it's not for me," I said, my voice loud enough to be heard over the music and waves of conversation emitted from the crowded dining room. "There's a little girl on the street. She's dirty and hungry and alone, and I'd like to take her a meal while I call for help. Are you telling me these people will be upset if you send an order for a sandwich or something to the kitchen while they wait an hour for their table?"

Conversation continued in the dining area, but those around us were silent. The manager, if that's what he was, glanced around at the waiting guests, his smile faltering for only a second before it blazed out stronger than before.

"Of course not, miss. We are always willing to help those in need. What can I get for you?"

I flipped through the menu again and pointed to a cheeseburger, thinking kids liked that kind of thing. To be safe, I ordered a salad and French fries to go with it and stood back when the manager slipped into the dining room. He handed the paper upon which he'd scribbled my order to one of the gorgeous servers who glided around the room and whispered something in her ear.

I stepped back from the podium, meeting the eyes of those who were watching me. Some looked annoyed, but a few smiled, nodding their approval. I glanced through the windowed door, searching the shadows for the little girl. At first, I couldn't see her, but then the shine of her eyes penetrated the darkness. There was no way to know she stared at me from such a distance and in the dark, but I was sure of it. I shuddered, wanting to get the food, give it to her, call the police, and make her someone else's problem.

The manager brought the bag of food to the little alcove and handed it to me with an even bigger and shinier smile than before.

"It's on the house. Get that little girl some help," he said loudly, for the benefit of everyone within earshot. People clapped as if he was some sort of hero, and I forced a smile when I took the bag from him. I thanked him graciously despite the fact I thought him a loathsome creature.

Back outside, with the warm, heavenly-scented bag clutched to my chest, I darted across the street. The little girl watched me from her garbage can cave, her eyes following me the entire way, which creeped me out. But I couldn't abandon the poor thing.

"Here, sweetie." I placed the bag in front of her. "It's a cheeseburger. And fries and a salad. I didn't know what you like, so I got some options for you."

The girl eyed the bag, but she didn't move to pick it up or open it.

"It's okay. It's for you. It's yours. You can take it."

She looked up at me and, as quick as a cat, grabbed the bag. She darted to the right and into the alley nearby.

"Wait!" I chased after her. The alley was dark, and I almost tripped more than once over debris scattered across the cement. I heard the little girl's quick steps ahead of me, but I couldn't see her in the shadows.

When I reached the other end of the alley, I paused and looked both ways, but she had vanished with her meal. Sighing in frustration, tinged with relief that she was no longer my problem, I hailed a cab and headed home.

***

Almost a week later, I saw the little girl again. This time, it was a bright afternoon, and she was huddled on a bench in the park. The park was a block from my house, and though part of me wondered if she had followed me home, the rational voice in my head told me there was no way she would have been able to chase the cab for over three miles the night I fed her. And how could she possibly know I jogged through this park a couple of times a week? My jogs didn't have a pattern since I never ran at the same time or on the same days each week.

She wasn't facing the path I used, so I only caught her profile when I neared, but she turned toward me, her eyes as haunting as they were the night we met. I stopped, suddenly wishing I had turned around the second I had seen her, but it was too late. She was staring at me, her eyes wide and glassy. Dirt on her face and

138

hands was embedded into every crease, deepening them to give her an ancient, withered look. She wore a dress, but her grimy feet were bare. She didn't show signs of recognition while she gazed at me, nor did she blink despite the breeze that shifted the filthy hair hanging past her shoulders.

Unable to pass her while she watched me, I strolled as casually as I could to the bench and crouched out of arm's reach. Though she had not threatened me in any way, something about her terrified me. I couldn't get the image out of my head of her throwing herself at me and biting me with brown and rotting teeth that I suspected hid behind her lips.

"Hello, again," I said softly, so as not to scare her.

She didn't respond, which wasn't a surprise after our last meeting. Bags under her eyes were made worse by dirt ground into the creases. When was the last time she'd slept?

"How did you get here? It's pretty far from the last place I saw you." I waited for an answer, but the girl maintained her silence. I frowned, searching her face for any sign she was listening to me, but other than the intense gaze, there was no movement or response. I sighed, reaching into my sweatshirt pocket and pulling out a granola bar.

She eyed the wrapped food, and her tongue peeked out again.

"Here, take this." I tore off the wrapper and held out the bar. She stared at it and looked at me again. When she didn't take the bar, I shifted my position to place it on the bench beside her. Her eyes followed the food, widening as I let it go. "I'm going to call someone to help you, to get you off the street. They'll take care of you, feed you. Okay?" Again, she stared at me, and I shrugged. I withdrew my cellphone and dialed 411, deciding a social worker would be better for this girl than the police.

As soon as I stepped away, the girl leapt off the bench and raced across the park.

"Hey! Wait!" I yelled, but she didn't stop. She disappeared into the trees, taking my granola bar with her.

***

"**S**top feeding her," my mother scolded during one of our weekly phone calls.

"She's just a kid, Mom." I rolled my eyes at her dismissal of this weird, needy child.

"A homeless kid. She's probably riddled with disease."

"You don't know that."

"Neither do you. Besides, she is obviously following you. Because you fed her. It's just like a stray dog, dear. Feed it once, and you'll never get rid of it."

"That's nonsense," I said. "She's not a dog; she's a kid. A little girl who needs help."

"You'll never get rid of her now. She'll be everywhere you look, with her hand out."

I didn't bother to tell my mother that the girl had never put her hand out nor asked for anything. Instead, I changed the subject to knitting and let my mother prattle about how hard it was to knit with her arthritis. I no longer had to listen to her. Instead, I mumbled "uh huh" once in a while until she wore herself out and hung up.

***

**T**wo days later, the girl appeared outside my house.

I was walking home from my friend's apartment, stumbling from the wine I'd consumed, and didn't see her until she appeared in front of me. Choking back a scream at the sight of her eyes peering at me through the gate, I tripped, landing hard on my behind. She was eye level with me, her dirty hands wrapped around the wrought-iron bars.

"What are you doing here?" I asked, my voice louder than I had intended.

She didn't flinch but looked through the gate. She was inside my gate. On my property.

"How did you find me? Are you following me?"

Her silence infuriated me, probably due to the wine and the fear of her sitting behind my gate, waiting for me to feed her. My mother's words echoed in my head, and I shoved them away.

The girl stared at me, seemingly unaware of my anger. I stood, reached over the gate, and unhooked the latch.

"Let go, please, so I can open it." I waited while her hands slid down the bars and dropped into her lap. Her head hadn't moved to follow me, but her eyes did. "I need you to back up, or the gate will hit you when I open it."

For the first time, without the offer of food, her body shifted. Her hands pressed down on the stone pathway and pushed. I cringed when her knees slid back on the rough stone and pictured the scrapes and cuts she must be enduring. When she was back far enough for me to enter, I swung open the gate and stepped inside. It closed behind me, and I stood before the girl, unsure what to do. Obviously, she felt an attachment to me due to the food I'd given her, but I didn't want to spend the rest of my life feeding her.

Had I been sober, I probably would have pulled out my cellphone and called the police, but the wine clouded the rational voice in my head. The way she stared at me and the filthy clothes and dirty face all dissolved my drunken anger into drunken sympathy.

"Come on," I said. "I've got food inside."

I climbed the steps, pulling the keys from my purse. Glancing back, I had my second shock of the night. She stood at the bottom of the stairs. Her eyes shone from the light above my door. She had followed me the ten feet to the stairs without making a sound. I shuddered, trying to unlock the door without taking my eyes off her, but I couldn't insert the key. Turning enough to see the lock, I jammed in the key and turned it harder than I needed to. Luck kept it from snapping in half, and I yanked it free, turning again to check on the girl.

She stood on the step directly behind me. She didn't touch me or say a word, only gazed at me with those haunting eyes. I reached back, turning the door handle. It slipped, and I realized my hands were sweating. Wiping my left hand on my pants, I grabbed the handle and tried again, this time succeeding. Keeping my eyes on her, I stepped over the threshold and held the door open for her.

"Come in," I said, hearing the tremor in my voice.

For some reason, seeing her step forward relieved me. It was such a normal thing to do, stepping into a house, that her weirdness seemed a little less odd. Maybe she was shy or frightened, as I was. That thought had never occurred to me, and I felt like an idiot, fearing a little girl who had done nothing but look at me funny.

"I can make you something to eat." I dropped my purse on the kitchen counter and hung my coat over the back of a chair. I rummaged through the fridge, trying to find something a kid would want. "How about some soup? It'll be nice and warm, since it's so cool out tonight."

The girl stood in the doorway of the kitchen, her eyes on mine, her eyebrows straight across her forehead, making it impossible to read her expression. Her hair hung around her face, and again I realized how dirty she was.

"You need a bath." My nose wrinkled at her smell. I hadn't noticed it outside in the fresh air, but within the confines of my home, the stench was like sweaty garbage. "I'll run you a bath, and your soup can heat while you soak." I motioned her to follow, and when she crept across the floor, I led her to the bathroom.

Though the bright light hurt my eyes due to my overzealous wine consumption, the girl didn't flinch. Again, I felt a twinge of fear at her unblinking eyes. I inserted the plug in the tub and turned on the water. I dumped into the tub more than double the recommended dose of scented bubble bath without asking whether she liked bubble baths. I left her in the bathroom while I went to the kitchen to heat the soup.

I turned the burner to low and returned to the bathroom. She stood beside the toilet, her eyes on me as soon as I appeared. I glanced at her and then checked the level of the water. It was about half full, more than enough for the kid to get clean.

"Okay, sweetie, take off your dress and climb in."

She didn't move. I pursed my lips, not wanting to touch her dirty clothing, but she made no effort to undress, so I undid the front buttons. She didn't stop me when I lifted the hem and pulled the dress over her head. She even raised her arms without prodding.

I helped her into the tub and placed a cloth on the side. She ignored it. Had she ever had a bath?

I sighed. "I'll help you."

It took almost half an hour to wash her hair and bathe her. The water was black when I was done, the bubbles unable to handle such a huge amount of filth. I had to leave her alone a couple of times to check the soup, but every time I returned, she was in the same position, her eyes following my every move.

I didn't have any kid-sized clothing, but I found a pair of shorts, which had a drawstring that could be tightened enough to fit her, and an old T-shirt that no longer fit me. The sleeves hung well past her hands, so I rolled them up until her hands were free.

We went to the kitchen, and I set a bowl of soup before her. Her tongue poked out between her lips. She didn't pick up the spoon but looked back and forth between me and the bowl.

"Can't run with this one, huh?" I smiled. "Guess you'll have to eat it here. It's okay. It's for you."

She slowly picked up the spoon and dipped it into the soup. Her eyes never left mine while she sipped and scooped up more. This unnerved me more than anything else she had done, so I left the room.

I needed to decide what to do. Social workers would have gone home for the night. The police were an option, but where would they take her? Would they put in a shelter or lock her in a cell? I cringed.

Peeking into the kitchen again, I saw she was finished eating. Her eyes were on mine the second I came into view, and I shuddered at what I was about to say. Did I actually want this silent thing in my house all night? Taking a deep breath, I nodded in answer to my question, knowing I couldn't put her back on the street.

"You can sleep here tonight, and I'll find someone to take you in tomorrow. A social worker can find you a safe place to live so you won't be on the street anymore. Does that sound all right with you?" I don't know why I asked her questions since she never answered them.

I beckoned her to the living room and helped her lay on the couch. I pulled a spare blanket from the closet and tucked a throw pillow under her head. She looked cozy cuddled under the woolen blanket, her clean brown hair spilling across the pillow. I smiled at the pretty face that had been camouflaged beneath the grime. I smiled, but she didn't smile back, which was fine.

"Go to sleep, sweetie. You're safe here."

I turned off the lights, glancing back when I headed to my bedroom.

Her wide eyes stared at me until I closed the door.

*** 

The first thing I saw when I woke up was the girl's eyes. They shone in the darkness, focused on me, barely two feet from my face. I screamed, clawing my way across the bed, as far from her as I could get. She didn't move but watched while I rolled out of bed and pressed myself against the wall on the other side of the room.

"What the hell are you doing in here?" I yelled.

She glared at me a moment and then turned away, looking out my now-open bedroom door. I couldn't see anything out there, but she gazed as if she saw something invisible to me.

"What is it? What did you do?" I asked, my heart pounding in my chest.

Then I heard it, a clinking sound of glass against glass. Someone, or something, was in my kitchen. I reached to my nightstand for my cellphone but remembered it was in my purse on the kitchen counter. I moaned, and the girl's head slowly turned back to me, her wide eyes bright in the darkness. She blinked, the first time she'd done that in my presence.

"She's hungry," she said, her voice a croak from lack of use.

"Who's hungry?" I remembered how the girl had darted away with the food I'd given her those first two times.

She didn't answer but faced the door when heavy footsteps crossed the kitchen, moving closer to the bedroom with each step.

144

A shadowy figure rose in the doorway. Long, stringy hair hung over its face. Eyes peered through the strands, staring at me. Even in the dim light, I saw the resemblance.

My mother had warned me about feeding strays, but she never mentioned they'd bring others to feed as well.

# WOMEN MUST STICK TOGETHER
## Cassandra Williams

**B**efore moving to the rental property in the country, Mona had looked forward to relaxing at night with the windows wide open, listening to limber branches sway or crusty leaves rustle. Crickets' chatter and water lapping at rocks in the nearby water garden would soothe her to sleep. The buzz of silence would prevail at other times, and she was positive she would hear the quiet, as crazy as that sounded.

Since moving, however, the only time she experienced peace in the evenings was inside the house, with the windows closed tight. Night noise rang in her ears then, a faint but discernible hum as if sounds floated like dust particles, which was better than the alternative when the windows were open.

Though savouring peace and solitude, she had enjoyed the rumblings from the trains that had lumbered down the tracks near her previous home in the city. Choruses of *clickety-clacks* and forlorn *woo-woos* had been oddly relaxing after a hard day's work, easing the stress of waiting tables and fending off obnoxious, horny men.

She lay coverless and naked on the bed. Temps must have surpassed thirty-five degrees Celsius, which had forced her to open the window. Perspiration covered her. The white curtains were as flimsy as the breeze, providing no relief from the heat even when unexpected whispers of air caused the gauzy material to billow.

For some odd reason, the occasional flapping resembled angel wings, probably because her mood had been the farthest side of angelic since relocating. The Miles' house and its occupants were within sight and sound, respectively, constantly ruining the nights. Nothing should mar the peacefulness of the countryside; nothing should intrude upon her little bit of heaven except nature's laughter.

Even in the city, living in a large apartment complex with neighbours above, under, and either side of her, she hadn't had to endure such nonsense. She would never have moved to the country had she thought a neighbour's commotion would constantly hinder her sleep. To drown out the Miles' screeching, she sometimes imagined trains in the distance. She was only fifty-eight kilometres away from the railroad tracks that ran by her previous home; surely she could hear them. And she did—if she pretended and strained hard enough. But that was only an auditory illusion.

Mona groaned. Though the heat had drained her strength, she brandished her arms and clenched her fists as if preparing to punch someone in the face. Maybe she would. Those dratted neighbours would pay for their sins, maybe sooner than later. If she had to put up with their wretched bitching much longer, she'd lose her cool, and who knew what would happen then. When her temper was incited, anyone within twenty feet of her best seek cover.

She'd never actually seen the couple—Mr. and Mrs. Miles— and only knew their surname from the real estate agent when she viewed the property she ended up leasing, which was located next to them. But she'd heard them spew cuss words enough to envision two frightful faces and bizarre bodies, a canvas that remained wet no matter how often the wind blew or how long it was left to dry in the sun.

She pictured Mr. Miles stomping through the house, a hairless head atop a blubbery body, with perspiring palms and feisty fists smashing everything in his way. Tiny and tired Mrs. Miles would be no match for her bruiser husband who, obviously, felt compelled to conquer women. Mona envisioned them in bed, too, the ancient bedsprings creaking under the brute's oppressive weight and the hapless woman beneath him, barely able to breathe. But all that was more depiction than Mona wanted to fathom. She didn't want to visualize repulsive couples copulating. And ugly they were; she was certain of that.

In Mr. Miles' defence, she figured Mrs. Miles had a bit of a mouth, compelling him to lay his hands on her. Mona heard Mrs. Miles' loud and piercing voice at nights when the couple was hard at it and couldn't fault the man for losing his cool, even though abuse against women wasn't right in any circumstances. She was a woman, after all; females must stick together against domineering males of the world, and she reprimanded herself for putting any blame on small and defenseless Mrs. Miles. But Mona herself had lost control in the past and had experienced the difficulty maintaining one's good nature when the world didn't particularly follow the path one desired.

"Enough already!" she screamed, throwing meandering thoughts aside and bounding out of bed. "I've had it. Truly had it!" She had it up to her eyeballs and beyond, farther even than her height of five foot four, at the nonsense she was forced to listen to night after night. And that night the racket was worse than usual—if that was possible.

She stumbled around in the dark, finally switching on the light and slipping into a pair of jeans—underwear be damned—and a T-shirt. She paused at the sudden velocity of the male voice and hoped she'd arrive in time to save the poor woman.

Mona didn't have a plan in mind, no inkling what she might do when she reached their house or how she'd subdue hefty Mr. Miles. But she had to do something. The pitiful, downtrodden woman needed help, and the nearest house was kilometres away, which left only Mona.

After a final glance about the bedroom, she went to the kitchen. The dozen or so knives, all different shapes, sizes, and severity, all recently honed to razor-blade thinness, leered at her from the under-counter fluorescent light. *Eeny meeny, miney, moe*, she thought. "Eeny, meeny, you're the one."

When she finished her singsong, she selected the largest of the knives, luckily the one her finger had landed on because that's the one she would have picked anyway. The thickest didn't necessarily make it the sharpest knife on the wall, but she'd need the largest against Mr. Miles—whether she did or didn't arrive in time.

*** 

**D**espite Mona's sticky clothing and the sweating she'd suffered earlier, the warmth of the night comforted her while she ambled across the field, flashlight in one hand, knife in the other. Once upon a time, the Miles' house had been the main house and hers the servants' quarters.

She had moved to the country because she didn't want to live in a cookie-cutter house or have houses flanking hers. She wouldn't have settled on 2329 Willow Wood Road had she known the sole neighbours were insufferable and unpleasant. With a narrow field and a fence separating the properties, she had thought a safe distance existed, enabling her to use discretion as to whether she'd consider the unknown couple true neighbours or not—as in, can-I-borrow-a-cup-of-sugar folk. She had never expected to hear their vile voices every evening, which afforded her zero chance of ever wanting to be friendly.

Though heavy, the knife seemed like a feather in her hand, whereas the small LED flashlight was dead weight. The shouting increased as she neared the house. A light shone from a front room, which Mona assumed was the living room.

She stepped on the wide front porch and peered in the large window. The room was awash with light, but no one was there. She still heard the man screeching, his voice thundering to the outdoors. She shivered. Rivulets of sweat dribbled from between her breasts as if insects slithered to her waist. She fanned her arms to allow circulation under her armpits.

Carefully, she opened the door, hoping the ancient hinges wouldn't give her away. She entered the hall and gently closed the door behind her. She peered to her left, which was, as she had suspected, the living room. To her right was another room, probably the parlour from what she could glean in the dim light.

The ruckus, still going strong, was happening on the second floor. The dark staircase was slightly illuminated by a shadowy light at the top of the stairs. From one of the bedrooms, she figured, for that's where they'd be. In the bedroom. In bed. Mr. Miles on top, crushing his wee wife beneath him. Mrs. Miles would be panting, trying to catch a breath, waiting for him to enter and finish the deed.

Mona reconsidered. No! They were squealing—or Mr. Miles was. They wouldn't be in the throes of passion nor would he be raping. The noise wasn't like that.

She crept up the worn, wide steps, hoping again that ancient creaks wouldn't announce her presence. But the couple was too rambunctious to hear a subtle noise from an intruder. The male voice, raspier and more spiked in person, was louder than any sound a female would make.

Mona reached the top of the stairs. Her armpits smelt worse than previously. She paused while more moisture gathered between her breasts. Her T-shirt was plastered to her back as if she'd been whipped, the blood gluing fabric to skin. Even her crotch felt moist, gooey even. If she found the couple in the middle of sex, she prayed she wouldn't be turned on by the repulsive sight. What would that say about her? She shuddered at the thought of enjoying such a gross spectacle.

The lit room was at the far end of the hall. She clutched the railing that continued from the staircase and wrapped to her left. She glanced down between the railing and the stairs and saw light from the living room. Taking baby steps, she slipped across the hardwood. She ignored three dark bedrooms, assuming two closed doors were a closet and a bathroom.

A sudden shriek by Mr. Miles caused her to jump and almost scream. Despite her anxiety, she clearly discerned snippets: "You bitch . . . take that . . . and this . . ." and heard slaps that could only be against Mrs. Miles' sallow face or her bony butt. Mona pictured red splotches, perhaps a tad of blood—maybe a lot of blood. Maybe the woman's nose had been broken. Maybe her lip cut or a tooth knocked to the floor.

150

How had Mrs. Miles put up with thrashings and horrid words lambasted at her? Mona had been told by the realtor that the couple had owned the property next door for at least thirty years, and since Mona had heard commotion the first evening after moving in, she figured the episodes had been occurring for a long time. Why hadn't the woman left? Mona knew that was easy for an onlooker to say. Life was hard, and only individuals living in those situations knew the severity. Women left when they were ready, not before. If they left before they were ready, they'd return to their abuser. Mona knew. And understood. No, she wouldn't judge the other woman. She probably shouldn't be helping her either. A stranger shouldn't intrude where she wasn't wanted, shouldn't intervene without being invited.

But mayhem every night! She had to do something. If not for Mrs. Miles, for herself—for Mona—so she could enjoy the peace she was entitled to.

She stood outside the last bedroom, from where light splayed into the hall, and wished she could block her ears from the piercing voice. She heard the woman's quiet voice acquiescing, "Yes, dear; sorry, dear," and the unmistakable sound of sobs. Tears would be rolling down the woman's cheeks, mixing into the blood and diluting it; and thick drops would be seeping into her dull grey hair or plopping to the compressed pillow.

Mona had heard enough. No female deserved that. To top it off, it sounded as though Mrs. Miles was compliant, as if used to the rampage, which ensured she would suffer again in the future. That wasn't right. Women must stand tall for all women even if a woman wasn't aware she was being damaged. Mrs. Miles was one of those unwitting individuals.

Mr. Miles' voice rose. "You damned well be certain you do. Say you're sorry again. I want to hear you grovel." He laughed then, a laugh from deep within a rotten soul.

Mona gripped the doorframe before peering into the room. The glare blinded her at first, and several seconds elapsed before she could see clearly. Not believing her eyes, she blinked. *What?*

She blinked again. And again.

She backed away from the door. The episode couldn't be playing out as she'd seen. She had been mistaken. The light played tricks.

She gulped and slowly exhaled to cleanse her lungs, to give her strength to view the scene another time.

After a few seconds, she peeked into the room again, proving her eyesight was excellent.

She turned and stared at the knife, the blade sharper than she had originally thought, grateful she had grabbed the biggest one; she would need it. Though the scene had presented itself for mere seconds, she couldn't mistake the actors and their roles. The people she'd just witnessed didn't match the ones she'd envisaged. Mrs. Miles, the central person etched firmly in her mind, was huge, more monstrous and macabre than Mona imagined any man could be. And Mr. Miles—well, she couldn't believe she'd been so wrong about him.

As if a zealous soldier on the first day at war, she charged into the room, the knife outstretched. The larger individual still ranted and the smaller one murmured meek okays, but Mona was oblivious to the words. Her mission had been to save a defenseless woman.

But was the woman defenseless?

Mr. and Mrs. Miles hadn't yet realized someone had entered the room. The heftier figure, with layers of fat folding upon each other, was bending over the figure on the floor. Their naked bodies glistened from the overhead lightbulb and the humidity and heat.

Mona gaped at the burly woman's boobs, immense breasts that swayed and brushed the hairless chest of the man below. The elongated masses ending with dark, large nipples reminded Mona of two upside-down chocolate-dipped ice cream cones.

Mr. Miles suddenly glimpsed Mona and managed to cover his genitals but not before she saw the tiny upright critter posed as if thumbing a ride. Mrs. Miles, noticing his eyes darting away from hers, turned. Her eyes flared when she saw Mona.

Mrs. Miles stood, ready to pounce like the rabid feline she was. Mona clenched the knife, moved toward the obese woman, and lashed at one mammoth breast. Mrs. Miles eyed the spurting blood and reached down to cover the gash.

Mr. Miles, still on the floor, remained motionless, his hands still cupping his privates. His forlorn eyes gazed at his wife. His lips slowly parted. Bubbles appeared before drool leaked from the corners of his mouth.

Mona leapt at the corpulent woman once more, who was obviously stunned, perhaps in shock. Mona slashed the left breast, causing the woman to release her right breast to comfort the other. Blood spurted uncontrollably. Her blubbery belly, with its rolls of fat, hung toward her knees. Mona couldn't see her pubic hair. Was she shaved? A decisive "no" went through her mind. A woman looking like that would never shave. How would she even find herself?

Mona revved back to life. Mrs. Miles was still alive and could smother Mona with one fleshy bat-winged arm. Without another thought, she plunged the knife into the grotesque gut again and again until the woman collapsed to the floor. The deafening noise, a tree-dropping-in-the-forest kind of sound, jarred Mr. Miles to attention. Forgetting his nudity, he stood, probably the fastest move he had made in years.

"Sweetie," he moaned. "Oh, my sweetie." He fell to his wife, his skeletal body barely covering one of her lumpy legs.

Despite her injuries, Mrs. Miles opened her mouth. "I'm here, I'm still here. Get that woman, you bitch! Get her!"

"What? Who? Me?" He scrunched his face and flailed his arms.

Mrs. Miles pushed her husband away, turned over, and heaved to all fours. Skin from her shredded, scarlet breasts swayed to the floor, blood pouring from her chest.

Without thinking, Mona dug the knife into the woman's butt, and Mrs. Miles screeched, one of those evil screams Mona had endured at night.

"Take that, *you* bitch," Mona yelled.

Mrs. Miles plunked to the floor, face first.

Mr. Miles sprang to action. He swatted at Mona and tried to wrestle the knife from her hand, but the thin, tiny man was no match for her. Mona plunged the knife into the side of his cheek, surprised to see the blade emerge out the other end. His eye sockets became perfect circles when realization dawned, yet the pain seemed to spur him on. When Mona withdrew the knife, he lunged at her again, and she thrust the sharp blade into his neck and withdrew it just as quickly. Blood spurted like a faucet flowing cherry juice. Dazed, he stood for several seconds, obviously uncomprehending until he touched his face as if to stop the flow. But it was useless. He collapsed a second later.

Mrs. Miles, still attempting to stand, was losing blood as fast as Mr. Miles had. But she had more weight, more blood to lose, more stamina. Mona wasn't taking any chances. She thrust the knife into the woman's neck as she had her husband. Mrs. Miles toppled and rolled to her back. Her breasts sagged to her sides and hit the floor. Her body looked as if someone had thrown a gallon of scarlet paint at her. "Sweetie . . ." she said, looking over at her husband.

Mona, forgetting she was supposed to stick up for women, attacked the defenseless creature again. In and out with the knife, in and out of the woman's belly. Mona figured her efforts were futile since the knife wouldn't reach vital organs through those many layers of flesh. Mrs. Miles continued to breathe, panting like a dog, huffing and whimpering and panting, each breath harder and harder.

Mona loomed over her as Mrs. Miles had stood over Mr. Miles. "How do you like it now, *sweetie*?"

Mona's sugary voice registered with Mrs. Miles; Mona knew it had. The almost-dead woman's eyes glistened. Blood spread from under her and across the hardwood to seep through the hundred-year-old cracks. Mona wondered if the blood would reach the ceiling of the main floor. Would it cause a red watermark on the ceiling? Would the old plaster eventually tear away and fall to the floor?

As if exhaling from a cigarette, the battered woman took one last puff. Mona watched, enjoying the sight. Previously, she hadn't thought she'd enjoy the evening, not after it had been so rudely interrupted, nor had she ever thought she'd enjoy a blood display. But she had. Could she do it again? She wasn't sure. Only if someone bothered her—horribly irritated her—then she supposed she could. Yes, she could. She was sure of it.

Mona hiked her T-shirt over her head, placed the knife on the fabric, and rubbed the damp material over the blade to remove her fingerprints. What else had she touched? The front door. The railing. That was it, wasn't it? She removed her jeans.

"Goodbye, Mr. and Mrs. Miles. I'm leaving. I'll have some peaceful sleep now." She snickered. "So will you."

While retreating, she rubbed her jeans along the second floor railing and down the stairs. She covered her right hand with the denim, opened the door, and wiped the outside knob after she closed it.

"Funny," she muttered while moseying home, "I still don't know their first names."

# SHEEP AND SNAKES
## Billy Lyons

The massive F-250 powered its way up the narrow, crooked highway that led into the tiny mountaintop town of Stony Ridge, Virginia. Behind the wheel sat Bobby Ray Simpson, longtime pastor of The Holy Tabernacle of Our Blessed Redeemer. Elizabeth Ann, his devoted wife of twenty-four years, cuddled close beside him.

Before long, Bobby Ray pulled off the roadway into a service station so quaint it could've been stolen off the set of *The Andy Griffith Show.* An earnest-looking young man wearing greasy brown overalls rushed to greet them.

"Good Morning, Pastor Simpson," he said, the words muddled by a syrupy Southern accent.

"Good Morning, James," Bobby Ray purred, stepping out of the truck.

"Fill her up?"

"Please."

James removed the gas cap and inserted the nozzle. "I've been meaning to thank you, Pastor, for everything you did in helping me get the appointment to West Point. I'm sorry I couldn't cut the mustard. I just got so gosh-darned homesick that I couldn't take it anymore."

"I suppose it's true what they say, James. There's no place like home. Anyway, no apology is necessary." Bobby Ray replied magnanimously. "I was glad to help."

The gas pump clicked off, and James removed the hose and slid it back into place. When Bobby Ray reached into his wallet for his Amex, James shook his head. "No sir, this one's on me."

"Why, thank you, James."

"Have a great day."

"I will." Bobby Ray climbed back into the truck. He turned the key and slammed the gas pedal to the floor. When the RPMs maxed out, he popped the clutch and peeled out, leaving burnt rubber and dirty exhaust in his wake.

Elizabeth Ann leaned over and kissed her husband's cheek. "I think it's just wonderful how you don't hold a grudge against James for dropping out of West Point. I know you went to a lot of trouble to get Senator Scott to nominate him."

Bobby Ray shrugged. "It just turned out that it wasn't in God's plan for him to become an army officer, after all." But he thought, *What else would you expect? James is no different than the rest of the stupid fucking sheep I'm forced to endure every day of my life. A little brighter than most perhaps, but stupid nonetheless.*

Bobby Ray Simpson was not a very nice man, but he came by his disposition honestly. As did many children who grew up in Stony Ridge, Bobby Ray had spent a great deal of his time poor and hungry. His father was a coal miner by trade, a profession as financially speculative as it was dangerous. It was boom or bust, with the boom times few and far between. Despite the bad times, Bobby Ray's mother managed to scrape up enough cash each month to send a love offering to the *Holy Power Hour* television broadcast. When Bobby Ray asked why she sent money to the TV preacher, she replied he was storing treasures in Heaven.

Bobby Ray had thought an occasional peanut butter sandwich would be much more valuable than any heavenly treasure, but said nothing since his mother's second favorite Biblical homily was "spare the rod, spoil the child."

While growing up, Bobby Ray quickly grew fascinated with the *Power Hour* and its long-time leader, Dr. D. Dwight Rutherford. How could one man command such blind loyalty? *They're just like sheep,* he thought with awe, *and he's their shepherd.*

From that day forward, every Saturday night Bobby Ray joined his mother on their tattered sofa and made an almost clinical study of D. Dwight Rutherford. The part he enjoyed most was the last fifteen minutes, a segment called "The Hotline to Heaven." It was during this grand climax that Rutherford delivered divine messages.

"Someone out there," Rutherford said one night, "is suffering from terrible, debilitating back pain. It is so severe that the poor soul who endures it grows more despondent with each passing day. This person truly believes that God no longer loves them. Let me tell you here and now that nothing could be further from the truth. God wants to free you, but your lack of faith ties His hands. You must show Him that you still believe, and God is telling me that the best way is to send in a love offering to the *Holy Power Hour*. Do it today, and be assured of deliverance tomorrow."

Even as a young boy, Bobby Ray recognized the genius of Rutherford's scheme. Out of the tens of thousands of viewers, there had to be at least a few with back pain so painful they would do anything (which included writing a check) to make it disappear. And once the check cleared the bank, their hard-earned money became property of the *Holy Power Hour*.

Once Bobby Ray had become familiar with Rutherford's tricks of the trade, he practiced preaching every time he had the house to himself, using his beloved border collie, Shep, as an imaginary viewer.

"Do you *believe*, Brother Shep? Do you *believe* that God's Holy Spirit can save your soul? Do you *believe* you can spend eternity in paradise? If you *believe*, Brother Shep, send your cash, check, or money order to me, Reverend Bobby Ray Simpson, care of this station. Do it today, and be assured of salvation tomorrow." Brother Shep must have *believed* because every now and then he licked his balls and barked, "Hallelujah."

Before long, Bobby Ray could imitate the TV preacher's message, diction, and delivery so perfectly it was scary. Then he began a comprehensive study of the Bible, which took precedence over everything else in his life.

Shortly after his twelfth birthday, Bobby Ray went to his pastor, the Reverend James Thompson.

"Hello, Bobby Ray." The elderly cleric smiled warmly when he motioned to the empty chair across from his desk.

Bobby Ray returned the pastor's smile and sat.

"What can I do for you?"

Bobby Ray got straight to the point. "Pastor Thompson, do you believe God can communicate through dreams?"

"The Bible teaches us that God is omnipotent, Bobby Ray. Do you know what that means?"

"It means that He can do anything He wants."

Pastor Thompson smiled again, more broadly this time. "You're right! God can do anything He wants, meaning He can certainly communicate with people through dreams."

"Even with someone as young as me?"

"Of course. Do you remember Joseph and his coat of many colors? He was just about your age when God spoke to *him* through a dream." He reached across the desk and put his hand on top of Bobby Ray's. "Did you have a dream that you believe came from God?"

Bobby Ray nodded. "I think so. I was walking all alone in the middle of a huge desert. There were no trees, no animals, nothing but the blazing sun. I knew I was going to die from heat stroke unless there was a miracle, and I was just about to lie down and die when I noticed something way off in the distance. At first I was afraid that it was one of those fake images that people sometimes see when they're in the desert. I can't remember what they're called."

"Do you mean a mirage?"

Bobby Ray nodded. "That's right, a mirage. I thought it was a mirage, but since I was going to die anyway, I figured I might as well die trying, so I gathered up my last little bit of strength and kept going. By the time I made it to what I thought was the mirage, I was so far gone that I was crawling on my belly like a snake. But you know what? Instead of a mirage, there was an oasis. In the center was a pond filled with the most beautiful-looking water I'd ever seen. I crawled up to the water's edge and started drinking. It was so clear and cold that I thought it would taste better than any water I'd ever had, but can you guess what happened, Pastor?"

"What happened?" The pastor's voice quivered with excitement.

"It tasted horrible! It looked like perfectly good water, but it tasted so bad that I couldn't swallow a single drop. Finally I just gave up and sat there feeling sorry for myself when I heard this mighty voice. Somehow, I just knew the voice belonged to Jesus."

"Hallelujah!" Pastor Thompson exclaimed.

Bobby Ray stood. "And this is what the Lord said to me: 'Bobby Ray Simpson, hear me well. The water is bitter because it has been contaminated by sin, a sin which would eventually spread throughout all mankind, if not for those blessed servants I have chosen to deliver my message. I have chosen *you*, Bobby Ray Simpson, to be one of these servants. Will you accept my calling and lead the people of Stony Ridge to the unspoiled waters?'"

Bobby Ray paused and looked directly into the pastor's eyes. "I know that I'm just a kid, but if the Lord has faith in me, then I should return that faith, no matter how young I am. So I just said yes. 'Yes, Lord,' I told Him, 'I will.' Then a bolt of lightning came down from Heaven and struck the pond right in the middle. I took another drink, and this time it was delicious. With each swallow I could feel the God's power pouring into me. When I stopped, I was filled with the Holy Spirit, from the top of my head all the way down to the soles of my feet. Once I'd drunk all the water, God spoke to me one last time. 'Go forth, Bobby Ray, and feed my sheep.'

"The next thing I knew, Mom was yelling for me to come down to breakfast. I opened my mouth to let her know that I'd heard her, but a Bible verse came out of my mouth instead. Now I'm ashamed to tell you, Pastor Thompson, that even though I'm twelve years old, I've never memorized one single word of God's Holy Scripture. But now I can pull almost any verse I want out of thin air, just as if I'd learned it myself."

Bobby Ray stood for a second time and placed his hand over his heart. "By awesome deeds in righteousness You will answer us, O God of our salvation. Psalms 65:5-7."

When he finished, Bobby Ray sat back down and held his breath. He'd only memorized four Bible verses, and if he was asked for more, the con would be over before it had even started.

But the pastor didn't ask for more. Instead, he fell to his knees in front of Bobby Ray, weeping openly. "What a blessed day! For so long now I've asked God to send someone worthy to lead my flock after I'm gone. Today the answer to my prayers has finally come, in the form of a beautiful twelve-year-old boy. Isn't our Heavenly Father wonderful?"

Bobby Ray hugged Pastor Thompson. "Yes, Pastor, He most certainly is." On the inside Bobby Ray was laughing his ass off. He had just corralled his first sheep.

The following Sunday, Pastor Thompson asked Bobby Ray to sit up front with him during the morning service.

"My dear friends, last week I witnessed a miracle. From time to time, one of our young people will drop by my office, usually to talk about the first pangs of puppy love, a fight with a little brother or sister, or something similar. So I wasn't surprised when Bobby Ray came to see me, but I was surprised to find out that he wanted to tell me about a message God gave him during a dream. I was skeptical at first, but the more I listened, the more I realized that God has chosen him to do great things. It is for this reason that I've asked him to deliver this morning's sermon." Pastor Thompson motioned to Bobby Ray. "Ladies and gentlemen, Mister Bobby Ray Simpson."

Bobby Ray stepped forward and delivered a sermon that would be talked about in Stony Ridge for years to come. When he'd finished, two things were certain. Everyone present was as convinced as their pastor that Bobby Ray had indeed received a divine calling. Bobby Ray's position as the future leader of The Tabernacle was secure.

Three years later, Pastor Thompson fell while getting out of the shower and shattered his hip. When he passed away from complications the following month, Bobby Ray was unanimously chosen as the Tabernacle's new pastor.

It wasn't long before surrounding communities heard about the teenage marvel. As Bobby Ray's reputation grew, so did his opportunities. He received job offers from several big-city mega churches, as well as a primetime spot on the prestigious Trinity Broadcasting Network, but he turned them all down. National prominence might bring worldwide fame and six-figure salaries, but along with them came vindictive ex-mistresses and investigative reporters.

One of Bobby Ray's responsibilities as pastor was to travel around Stony Ridge with Elizabeth Ann to visit his parishioners. This morning their destination was the sprawling farmhouse inhabited by Walter and Mary Blankenship. After Bobby Ray parked the Ford, he and Elizabeth Ann walked to the front door and knocked. Instantly there came a cacophony of dogs barking and children yelling.

"Stevie!" A female voice boomed from within. "Pick up your toys, and take your brothers and sisters outside to play!" Soon a harried, but pretty woman opened the door. "Pastor!" She offered her hand, which Bobby Ray took in both of his and shook warmly. "Please come in, if you can clear a path. I'm always yelling at the kids to pick up their toys, but sometimes I think I just do it to hear my own voice, for all the good it does."

"It looks just fine," Bobby Ray lied, almost tripping over an Iron Man figure when he stepped inside.

"Please have a seat. The coffee should be just about ready." Mary walked into the kitchen to check the pot.

"Wonderful," Elizabeth Ann replied. "I haven't had a cup all day."

Minutes later, Mary returned with the coffee.

Bobby Ray sipped and smiled. "I love a woman who isn't afraid to make a strong pot of coffee."

"Walter likes his strong, so I guess I just got used to having mine the same way," Mary said.

"So tell me, Mary, how have you and Walter been?"

"We're blessed, Pastor. Walter is working so much overtime these days that I think his foreman sees him more than I do, but it's a nice problem to have. So many of the coal mines are laying people off or shutting down completely. The Lord has been so good to our family."

"Amen!" Bobby Ray and Elizabeth Ann said simultaneously and laughed.

Bobby Ray punched his wife lightly on the shoulder. "Jinx."

Elizabeth Ann rubbed her shoulder. "Are you guys going to be able to go anywhere for summer vacation?"

"Oh, yes!" Mary squealed with delight. "Let me show you." She opened the coffee table drawer and took out some brochures. She handed them to Bobby Ray and Elizabeth Ann. "Last week we sent in a down payment for our Disney vacation."

"How wonderful," Elizabeth Ann said. "I have to tell you, Mary, I'm jealous."

"I can't believe it's only six weeks away." Mary pointed to a picture of a child standing in front of a huge window. Just beyond the glass sat a lioness and her three cubs. "Our hotel is on the grounds of The Animal Kingdom, and it's designed so that the animals can walk right up to the rooms."

Bobby Ray frowned. "Oh, Mary, please tell me that your down payment is refundable."

"I'm not sure, Pastor. Why do you ask?"

"Well, it's just that the Southern Baptists have been boycotting all Disney parks for several years now. I know The Tabernacle isn't Baptist, but in this case I agree with them. Some of these Disney movies are downright blasphemous. And the way they make it a point each year to celebrate the Sodomites! Gay Days, I believe they call it. I just don't see how anyone who claims to be a Bible-believing Christian could spend even one day inside a Disney Park. *Do you?*"

For a second, a shadow darkened Mary's face, and Bobby Ray saw a tear. Mary forced it back and managed to smile.

"Of course not, Pastor. Walter and I didn't know about the boycott or the Gay Days." The joy, present in her voice mere moments previously, had become a lifeless monotone. "I'll tell Walter as soon as he comes home. Hopefully we can get our money back. Thank you."

Bobby Ray took Mary's hand. "You're more than welcome. That's what I'm here for, after all."

*Sometimes,* Bobby Ray thought, *it's fun to fuck with the sheep.*

Elizabeth Ann said nothing while they walked back to the truck. Once inside, Bobby Ray turned to her. "You got quiet all of a sudden. Is something wrong?"

Elizabeth Ann shook her head. "No. I just feel so bad for Walter and Mary."

"So do I," Bobby Ray said. "But—"

"I know. We're all so lucky to have you to help us make the right decisions."

"I'm the one that's lucky," Bobby Ray replied and started the truck.

"So where are we off to next?" Elizabeth Ann asked.

"I thought if it was okay with you, I'd head over to Jenny's. She wanted me to help her with her senior research before she goes back to Bible College next week. I'll get her to give me a ride back home."

Bobby Ray turned onto a dirt road and drove until he came to a red and white double-wide. When he climbed out, Elizabeth Ann slid over and took the wheel. "Have a good time. I'll have dinner ready when you get home."

When Elizabeth Ann arrived home, the first thing she noticed was the answering machine's blinking red light. She punched PLAY.

"Pastor Simpson, this is Amy Douglas at WVVA in Bluefield," the recorded voice announced. "My boss just gave me the green light to film your worship service this weekend. If you could give me a call at your earliest convenience, we can go over the details."

Elizabeth Ann smiled and thought, *Won't Bobby Ray be pleased. He's wanted this for so long.* She started toward the kitchen, but then stopped. She should go back to Jenny's and give him the good news.

Once she arrived at Jenny's trailer, Elizabeth Ann knocked hard on the front door, but there was no answer. She opened the door and stuck her head inside. "Bobby Ray? Jenny?" *Where can they be? Jenny's car is in the driveway, so they have to be around here somewhere.*

Elizabeth Ann walked down the hallway. She almost turned to leave when she heard voices. She approached the open door. She pulled back sharply.

Jenny lay on the bed, as naked as the day she was born. Bobby Ray, also naked, was on top of her.

"Oh, Pastor," Jenny said breathlessly. "You most certainly do know how to take care of your flock."

"Did I ever tell you I've been given the gift of tongues?" He took the first two fingers of his right hand and raised them like a peace sign, and then stuck his tongue in the middle and wiggled it wildly.

"I don't believe you," Jenny giggled. "Prove it."

"My pleasure," Bobby Ray purred and went down south. Seconds later, muffled exclamations came from the depths of Jenny's nineteen year-old honeypot. After a while he came up for air. "Shama-lama-ding-dong," he said and went back to work. "A whop-bob-a-lou-bop, a-whop-bam-boom!"

"Oh, Pastor! You really *do* have the gift of tongues," Jenny said.

Elizabeth felt the walls closing in, everything going black. She sunk to her knees and covered her mouth with both hands. When the screams from inside the bedroom became too much, she forced herself to return to the truck. Only when she was inside with the windows rolled up did she allow herself to cry. Bitter, agonizing tears. Eventually a semblance of composure returned, and she drove home.

She sat on the couch, expecting to cry again, but there were no more tears. "So," she said to no one in particular, "it's all just a bunch of bullshit. *Fucking bullshit.*" It was the first time she'd even thought the F-word, much less said it.

"So, Bobby Ray, what else have you been hiding from me?" She entered Bobby Ray's study, sat at his desk, and flipped on his PC. Once it booted up, she scanned the desktop for suspicious folders. One was labeled INVOICES. She double-clicked the icon, but the file didn't open. Instead, a small window appeared that asked for a password.

"Goddammit," Elizabeth Ann muttered. "How in the hell should I know his password?" She was about to give up and try again later when it came to her. She typed SHEEP, clicked the OK button, and the folder opened. She quickly found what she was looking for. "Gotcha!"

The next day, Elizabeth Ann made the fifty-mile journey to Bluefield, West Virginia. A couple of miles past the city limits, she arrived at her destination, a three-storey Victorian. A wooden sign beside the front door read Dr. Wesley Hutchinson, DVM. She entered. The office was empty, as she'd guessed it would be. Dr. Hutchinson was getting along in years and not far from retirement.

"Doctor Hutchinson?" It wasn't long before she heard someone coming down the steps.

Dr. Hutchinson smiled at Elizabeth Ann. For an elderly man, he had managed the stairs with ease and looked much younger than his seventy-six years. "How good it is to see you. Is Bobby Ray with you?"

Elizabeth Ann offered her hand. "No, he couldn't make it, but there's something that I do need to talk with you about, if you can spare a few minutes."

The old man gestured toward the empty waiting room. "I have nothing *but* time these days, but even if I didn't, I would make some for you, Elizabeth Ann. How about a cup of coffee?"

"A cup of coffee sounds just wonderful," Elizabeth Ann said and followed Hutchinson upstairs.

A couple of minutes later, they sat in the dining room, steaming cups of coffee in tow. Dr. Hutchinson smiled. "At the risk of sounding like a broken record, it really *is* good to see you."

"I hope you feel the same way once I tell you why I came. I found the invoices you send Bobby Ray every month."

Dr. Hutchinson's smile turned upside down. He tried to lift the coffee cup a second time, but his shaking hands prevented it. Elizabeth Ann placed her hands over them.

"It's okay, Wes. I know what a good man you are. No one could convince me otherwise. I think I understand what the invoices are for, but I need you to confirm it for me." She told him her suspicions.

The doctor's eyes filled with tears and he nodded. "Do you remember when Bobby Ray and I went to the Promise Keepers Conference in Huntington?"

"I think so. It was back in '94, wasn't it?"

"Exactly. Well, on the last night of the conference, we went to the hotel restaurant for dinner, and the next thing I remember it was the next morning. I was lying in bed, completely naked, with no recollection of anything that had happened after we sat down to eat. Bobby Ray walked in with a handful of Polaroids that showed me in bed with two hookers. He said he would give them to Emily if I didn't do as he asked. I couldn't let that happen. It would have killed her."

"I understand completely," Elizabeth Ann said. "Believe me, you're not the only one guilty of drinking the Bobby Ray Simpson Kool-Aid. I've been gulping it down for almost twenty-five years. He's a terrible man, and now, thanks to you, I can stop him."

"Is there anything I can do to help?"

She leaned in close.

***

The following Sunday was standing room only at The Tabernacle. Men, women, and children in the crowded pews fidgeted while they waited for the last part of the service. The WVVA news crew stood in the back of the sanctuary, filming the service.

During the offertory, Bobby Ray sat behind the altar, his hands raised toward Heaven as the organist played "Bringing in the Sheaves." At the end, the deacons marched forward with the offering plates, each one overflowing with checks and cash.

Once the deacons took their seats, Bobby Ray stood and smiled at the camera. *Maybe it was a mistake to turn down the TV offers,* he thought. *Maybe others are dumb enough to get caught, but I'm Bobby Ray Simpson, smarter than your average televangelist. I'll give TBN a call in the morning.*

Bobby Ray cleared his throat. "Now we come to the most important part of our service, which is based on the words of the Apostle Mark: 'And these signs shall follow them that believe. . . . They shall take up serpents; and if they drink any deadly thing, it shall not hurt them; they shall lay hands on the sick, and they shall recover.'

167

"There are those who would tell you that these words have no relevance in today's society, but at The Tabernacle we do not believe the Bible is time sensitive. Instead, we consider each word inerrant. So, on every first Sunday of the month, we boldly proclaim our faith in the Lord Jesus Christ. For thirty years we have handled serpents at the Tabernacle, and in those thirty years not one member of our congregation has been bitten. I promise that as long as your faith in me remains strong, no one ever will. I will now ask our elders to do their duty."

Bobby Ray sat back down and smiled. How easy it had been to blackmail the broken-down country vet into providing a fresh batch of snakes each month. The copperhead might be one of the most dangerous serpents in the country, but Doc Hutchinson removed their venom glands each week before the service, so even if one did bite, nothing would happen. Furthermore, there was almost no chance that a snake would strike because Hutchinson also gave them Isobutene, a drug that rendered them so sluggish they could barely move.

Moments later, the elders came forward with a large wooden box and placed it on top of the altar. The box was held shut by a heavy iron padlock. The chief elder handed a key to Bobby Ray, who unlocked the box and returned the key

After the elders returned to their seats, Bobby Ray lifted his arms toward Heaven. "Heavenly Father, I ask that You bless me, Your faithful servant, for my good works and steadfast faith in You." He reached inside the box, grabbed two handfuls of snakes, and held them up to the crowd.

Within a second, Bobby Ray realized he was seriously fucked. The snakes, normally docile to the extreme, writhed inside his grip with strength he had never felt before. One bit the soft flesh just below his right cheek and hung there, writhing and emptying its venom. Bobby Ray didn't feel pain at first, but soon the poison did its work, and he screamed. "It hurts! Oh, dear God, how it hurts!"

Then another copperhead sprang forward and landed dead center in Bobby Ray's left eye. The snake's considerable weight strained against his orbital bone, and the resulting pull, along with the reptile's frenzied undulations, caused Bobby Ray's eye to pop out of its socket. It fell a few centimeters before being stopped by the optic nerve that connected it to his brain. While Bobby Ray stood screaming with two copperheads hanging from his face, the three that remained also attacked. Two bit all the way through his tongue, and the last landed on the bridge of his nose.

Bobby Ray howled and hopped in place, looking like Medusa—if Medusa had ever been hit in the face with a shovel. With Bobby Ray's remaining good eye, he looked wildly around the sanctuary, searching in vain for any kind of savior. Eventually his glance fell on Elizabeth Ann, sitting in the front row beside Doc Hutchinson. *But that makes no sense,* he thought. *Elizabeth Ann always sits in back, and the old man hasn't been to church in twenty years.*

Elizabeth Ann and Doc Hutchinson smiled and raised their first two fingers in the air. Then they stuck out their tongues and made the international sign of cunnilingus.

The truth finally dawned on Bobby Ray. "You bitch. You fucking bitch," he tried to say, but with two snakes stuck to his tongue it came out, "Ew bith! Ew fudding bith!" His unintelligible curses continued for the next ninety seconds or so, which was all the time it took for the venom to render him unconscious. After another minute, his bloated, bloody face stared toward a Heaven he would never see.

Far below, Satan smiled. *Another sheep coming home.*

# THE AUTHORS

**Chantal Boudreau** – Chantal has been published in Canada with Exile Editions in their *Dead North* and *Clockwork Canada* anthologies. Other Canadian publications include stories in *Postscripts to Darkness Volume 5*, *Masked Mosaic: Canadian Super Stories,* and *Out of the Cave*. Outside of Canada, to date, she has published more than fifty speculative fiction stories with a variety of American and British publishers.

**Amanda Crum** – Amanda is a writer and artist whose work has appeared in publications such as *Dark Eclipse*, *SQ Magazine*, and *Blue Moon Literary & Art Review*. She currently lives in Kentucky with her husband and two children.

**L.S. Engler** – L.S. writes from outside of Chicago in the company of two cats and a boyfriend. She loves anything with a bit of magic in it and is currently finishing up a zombie project called *The Slayer Saga*. Her work has most recently appeared in *Ghostlight*, *Potter's Field Six*, and the *Saturday Evening Post* online.

**R.A. Goli** – R.A. is an Australian writer of horror, fantasy, speculative, and erotic horror short stories. She likes to pretend she writes sci-fi too, but just because she puts a robot in a story doesn't make it so. Her interests include reading, gaming, the occasional walk, and annoying her dog, two cats, and husband. Her short stories have been published by Deadman's Tome, Grivante Press, and Fantasia Divinity among others. Check out her website **https://ragolifiction.wordpress.com/** or stalk her on Facebook **https://www.facebook.com/ragolifiction**.

**Kev Harrison** – Kev is a thirty-seven-year-old English language teacher and writer, living in Lisbon, Portugal. He specialises in dark fiction and has had his work published in Jitter Press, several competition anthologies, and has recently had work selected for an upcoming anthology by Lycan Valley Press.

**S.T. Himmonds** – S.T. lives alone in the wilderness, void of all human contact, which is the way he/she enjoys life. You cannot find S.T. on the Wide Wild Web or via social media. Don't even try!

**S.D. Hintz** – S.D. has professionally published several short stories and a novel through small presses such as Black Bed Sheet Books, Dark Scribe Press, Lyrical Press, and several others. He recently sold his short story "Bellows" to Vagabondage Press for an upcoming anthology due for release in 2017. He is also the former Editor-in-Chief of KHP Publishers.

**Tom Johnstone** – Tom lives with his family in Brighton, England, where he works as a gardener for the local authority. He developed a taste for the macabre as a child in the Seventies watching TV shows like *Doctor Who* and *Sapphire and Steel*. Then he found a copy of H.P. Lovecraft's *The Lurking Fear and Other Stories* in his parents' bookshelf. The idea of writing his own horror stories didn't occur to him until much later, but now he's trying to make up for lost time! His fiction has appeared in the *Ninth*, *Tenth* and *Eleventh Black Books of Horror* (Mortbury Press), *Brighton – The Graphic Novel* (Queenspark Books), *Supernatural Tales* #27 & #31, *Terror Tales of the Scottish Highlands* (Gray Friar Press), *Strange Tales* V (Tartarus Press), and *Best Horror of the Year* #8 (Nightshade Books).

**Billy Lyons** – Billy's short story "Cell 334" was published in the November 2014 edition of *Another Realm* e-zine. His short story "Black-Eyed Children, Blue-Eyed Child" was published in

*High Strange Horror*, an anthology released in April 2015 by Muzzleland Press, where he is a contributing writer of book and movie reviews. His debut novel, *Blood and Needles,* was recently acquired by Intrigue Publishing and is scheduled for release in June 2017. He possesses B.A. and M.A. degrees in psychology from The Citadel and George Mason University, respectively.

**Shelly Macaroy** – Shelly Macaroy is a fictional character in the award-winning novel *Diaries of Karma (DOK)*, written by Bertram Allan Mullin, which won in the 2015 WILDsound competition and was a finalist piece in The Writers' League of Texas Manuscript Competition in 2014. Actor Geoff Mays read a chapter of the book online. Much like the author of DOK, Shelly has studied creative writing, has several publications including the horror "Bikutimu," which appears in the *Bride of Chaos Anthology* available on **amazon.com**. Shelly lives with her equally fictional girlfriend in Austin, TX. To find out about the author, go here: BAMWrites.com

**Leslie Muzingo** – Leslie grew up in Iowa but relocated to the Deep South some years ago. She has recently begun spending her summers in Prince Edward Island and finds great similarities between PEI and the rural Iowa of her youth. She was published in last year's Iowa State Writers Guild, *The World Retold* (2016). Her stories have also been found in *Literary Mama* (2015) and *Puff Puff Prose Poetry and a Play* (2015). She considers herself an emerging writer. Her emergence is a slow one as she has so many things she likes to do, and there are only so many hours in a day.

**Leah O'Sullivan** – Leah is a recent college graduate with a B.A. in English and a minor in gender studies. She has had prose and poetry works published in *CrossCurrents Literary & Arts Magazine* and in *Wetlands Magazine*, and has received the Esther Wagner Fiction Award for her short story, "The Dying." She is currently considering MFA programs while working as an administrative intern.

**Boyd Reynolds** – Boyd is a freelance writer and educator living in Vancouver, Canada. He has published short stories for children, teenagers, and adults. His other published works include newspaper articles, educational non-fiction pieces, and pop culture commentary. Boyd works as a librarian, holds a Master of Arts in Children's Literature and enjoys all things scary.

**Robb T. White** – Robb lives in Northeastern Ohio; since 2011, he has published a dozen short stories and three hardboiled private-eye novels featuring series character Thomas Haftmann. He also has over a dozen short stories of crime published in various webzines or print. He has one collection of short stories ('Out of Breath' *and Other Stories*, Red Giant, 2013), and a crime novel *When You Run with Wolves* (Number Thirteen, 2013). His ebook crime novel, *Special Collections*, won the New Rivers Electronic Book Competition in 2014. His latest Haftmann novel is *Nocturne for Madness* (New Pulp, 2016) and a forthcoming collection of crime stories is *Dangerous Women: Stories of Crime, Mystery, and Mayhem* to be published by Class Act Press.
Website: **http://tomhaftmann.wixsite.com/robbtwhite**.

**Cassandra Williams** – Cassandra, hoping to not be discovered, lives her dream in a modern cabin in dense woods, where she writes fiction and ponders a different and better world. She has had a variety of fiction published online and in print. Six cats, computer, and internet keep her sane.

**Monique Youzwa** – Monique is a ghostwriter with dozens of nonfiction articles published on various blogs online. Though she's been writing fiction for a number of years, she has only recently begun to seek publication for her various short stories. Though horror is her main focus, she's also at work on a fantasy novel and has recently written two children's stories. She's spent the majority of her life living in the same small town, currently with her husband and daughter.

# SOCIAL MEDIA LINKS
## MacKenzie Publishing

MacKenzie Publishing Website—
**https://mackenziepublishing.wordpress.com/**

*TWO EYES OPEN* Facebook page—
**https://www.facebook.com/twoeyesopen/**

*OUT OF THE CAVE* Facebook page—
**https://www.facebook.com/Out-of-the-Cave-1668695366743672/**

Writing Wicket Facebook Page—
**https://www.facebook.com/writingwicket/**

\*\*\*

For editing, formatting, and/or publishing,
contact MacKenzie Publishing at
**writingwicket@gmail.com.**
\*\*\*

*OUT OF THE CAVE*
*https://www.amazon.com/Out-Cave-stories-Stephen-Millard-ebook/dp/B01ICAWBVU/*

*TWO EYES OPEN*
https://www.amazon.com/Two-Eyes-Open-C-MacKenzie-ebook/dp/B0746NXNXW/

\*\*\*

If you enjoyed *TWO EYES OPEN* (or if you didn't!),
please leave a review.
Thank you!

Printed in Great Britain
by Amazon